Rise of the Pendragon

The Last Pendragon Saga:
The Last Pendragon
The Pendragon's Blade
Song of the Pendragon
The Pendragon's Quest
The Pendragon's Champions
Rise of the Pendragon

The Lion of Wales series:
Cold My Heart
The Oaken Door
Of Men and Dragons
A Long Cloud
Frost Against the Hilt

The Gareth and Gwen Medieval Mysteries:
The Bard's Daughter
The Good Knight
The Uninvited Guest
The Fourth Horseman
The Fallen Princess
The Unlikely Spy
The Lost Brother
The Renegade Merchant

The After Cilmeri Series:
Daughter of Time (prequel)
Footsteps in Time (Book One)
Winds of Time
Prince of Time (Book Two)
Crossroads in Time (Book Three)
Children of Time (Book Four)
Exiles in Time
Castaways in Time
Ashes of Time
Warden of Time
Guardians of Time
Masters of Time

Book six in *The Last Pendragon Saga*

RISE
of the
PENDRAGON

by

SARAH WOODBURY

To Taran

Pronouncing Welsh Names and Places

Aberystwyth –Ah-bare-IHST-with (the 'th' is soft as in 'forth')

Bwlch y Ddeufaen – Boolch ah THEY-vine (the 'th' is hard as in 'they'; the 'ch' as in in the Scottish 'loch')

Cadfael – CAD-vile

Cadwallon – Cad-WA/SH/-on

Caernarfon – ('ae' makes a long i sound like in 'kite') Kire-NAR-von

Dafydd – DAH-vith (the 'th' is hard as in 'they')

Dolgellau – Doll-GE/SH/-eye

Deheubarth – deh-HAY-barth

Dolwyddelan – dole-with-EH-lan (the 'th' is hard as in 'they')

Gruffydd – GRIFF-ith (the 'th' is hard as in 'they')

Gwalchmai – GWALCH-my ('ai' makes a long i sound like in 'kite; the 'ch' like in the Scottish 'loch')

Gwenllian – Gwen-/SH/-an

Gwladys – Goo-LAD-iss

Gwynedd – GWIN-eth (the 'th' is hard as in 'the')

Hywel – H'wel

Ieuan – ieu sounds like the cheer, 'yay' so, YAY-an

Llanbadarn Fawr – /sh/an-BAH-darn vowr

Llywelyn – /sh/ew-ELL-in

Maentwrog – Mighn-TOO-rog

Meilyr – MY-lir

Owain – OH-wine

Rhuddlan – RITH-lan (the 'th' is hard as in 'the')

Rhun – Rin

Rhys – Reese

Sion – Shawn (Sean)

Tudur – TIH-deer

Usk – Isk

1

Cade

"**Y**ou're telling me there are thirteen of these things to worry about?" Cade sat on the edge of a work table, with Dafydd beside him. Every now and then, Dafydd reached out a hand to touch the hilt of Caledfwlch. Cade had made it clear that he was to stay close and use it if he needed it. Goronwy had brought Dafydd in time, and Cade had healed his wound, but Dafydd still didn't feel quite right. None of them—not Cade, Dafydd, or Taliesin—could explain it.

Just as with the black shadow in the cavern beneath Dinas Bran.

Cade glanced at Taliesin, whose expression was unreadable. Now that he could *see* again, Cade had been able to get even less out of him than before, about the shadow or anything else.

"That is my belief," Taliesin said, answering the one question Cade had asked out loud. "You won't like the rest of the story any better."

"Better tell us quick, then." Goronwy peered through the slit between the door and the frame. They had gathered in a storage shed off the courtyard. "Rhys will be noticing you're gone and start to wonder."

Cade had included the two women, Angharad and Catrin, in the consultation: Angharad because for generations her family had owned the cloak she'd brought and she deserved to have a say in its future, and Catrin because ... well ... because Taliesin thought he should.

Cade too eyed the door. He'd arrived with Taliesin and his *teulu* the previous evening. The other lords of Wales had trickled in over the course of the day, but by the time the sun had set, the trickle had become a flood. Rhys and his men, Geraint and the lords of southern Gwynedd, with their knights and archers, and then a hundred others had arrived to fill the fort and its surrounding plateau with men. Only Rhun and Tudur were still missing. Cade was hugely relieved to know that he would have men to counter the Saxons. He'd called a Council session for within the hour.

Cade had chosen Caer Fawr as the place to meet because of its extensive defenses, its access to water close to the fort, and its proximity to Shrewsbury. He hoped the Saxons had never read Tacitus, for it was this spot that Caratacus had chosen for his last stand against the Romans. The fort was naturally defended such that they could cover every entrance and exit, with steep slopes on all sides and rings of an ancient rampart and ditch system of which Cade intended to take full advantage.

Caer Fawr had once been a great fortress, but now like Dinas Bran, lay half in ruins. The curtain wall, which followed the natural shape of the mountain, was one of the few works of stone that remained and enclosed a space of nearly three acres. In addition, a fifty-foot-wide extension at the southern end of the complex took up the base of the hill. Cade had posted watchers there and had ordered others to continually circle the mountain. If the Saxons came, Cade would know.

"The tale begins and ends with Arianrhod." Taliesin leaned on his staff, both hands clasped at the top and his chin resting on his fists.

Cade crossed his arms across his chest, prepared to be annoyed. "As it always seems to these days."

"As you say." Taliesin gestured to the items on the table. "These are some of the Thirteen Treasures of Britain which she kept, at one time or another, in her home on the

Isle of Glass. Some of them she commissioned, some she merely acquired or inherited."

"I know this story," said Dafydd. "It includes a prophecy about one who will gather the Treasures and in so doing, restore the Welsh to their former glory. To a time before the Romans came."

"Is that why Mabon wants them?" Angharad said. "Because he sees himself as a savior of the Welsh?"

Taliesin moved his head noncommittally. "His desire would be the power the Treasures would bring him."

"Of course it would," said Goronwy. "How could it not?"

"With every Treasure he collects, his power grows. He wouldn't even need to gather them all to find himself ruling not only the human world, but the world of the *sidhe*."

"Ah," Cade said. "Understanding dawns at last. Mabon is in the human world because the Treasures are here. But it's power among his own kind that he wants."

Dafydd shifted beside Cade. His hand went to Caledfwlch's hilt and he held it as he spoke. "No wonder the gods are taking sides. Do they know what Mabon has in mind? How many of the *sidhe* are with him and want him to overthrow Beli, who rules the *sidhe* council?"

Almost imperceptibly, Taliesin lifted one shoulder. "I'm not privy to those answers."

"So what are they, these Treasures?" Cade said. "Do you have a list?"

Taliesin licked his lips, glanced once at Cade, and recited just loud enough so that everyone in the hut could hear:

"Dyrnwyn, the flaming sword, lost for centuries beneath the earth.

A hamper that feeds a hundred, a knife to serve twenty-four,

A chariot to carry a man on the wind,

A halter to tame any horse he might wish.

The cauldron of the Giant to test the brave,

A whetstone for deadly sharpened swords,

An entertaining chess set,

A crock and a dish, each to fill one's every wish,

A drinking horn that bestows immortality on those worthy of it,

And the mantle of Arthur.

His healing sword descends;

Our enemies flee our unseen and mighty champion."

Silence descended upon the companions. Cade's hand clenched around a husk of bread, which he'd brought with him from the meal he'd interrupted to confer with his friends. As had become common of late, he was hungrier than he felt comfortable admitting, though that was far better than gaining energy by killing.

Goronwy broke the silence. "Why all the secrecy on Mabon's part? This foolishness with *it*. Why not name them?"

"Because naming has power?" Taliesin said. "Because he knows to whom the items were given, but not which Treasure each man possessed? His motivations remain a mystery to me, beyond that he seeks these items for his own power."

"Well, if they're a mystery to you, I don't see how we can hope to understand him," Cade said.

"Maybe we shouldn't try," Dafydd said.

Goronwy cleared his throat. "So, at this juncture, King Cadwaladr has collected Caledfwlch, the mantle, the knife, and the whetstone. Four of thirteen, since the fake Dyrnwyn doesn't count."

"So it seems," Taliesin said.

"All of which Mabon is seeking and because of Mabon, we now possess these in one place," Dafydd said.

"Again, yes," Taliesin said.

"None of this helps us in the slightest against the Saxons," Bedwyr said.

"No," Cade said. "The treasures comprise a separate issue, unless we have to fight Mabon for them at the same time as we fight the Saxons for our freedom."

"I hope that is not the case," Taliesin said. "Time is not the same to Mabon as to us. He's just as likely to disappear for a week as to know where we are and *when* it is to us."

"And Mabon isn't as powerful as he thinks he is," Dafydd said. "He's not a good swordsman. For all that he injured me, it was his sword that did the damage, not some invincibility or strange power of his own. He can't hurt you unless you let him and give him power over you. I don't understand him at all. I don't understand the world of the *sidhe* at all."

"Probably better that you don't," said Geraint.

"Perhaps his only real power stems from his association with his mother or father, and since neither are aware of his activities, he has only his *glamour* to fall back on," Dafydd said.

"He can do a lot with *glamour*," Goronwy said.

Geraint jerked his chin towards the door. "It's time to go."

"Just a moment." Cade gazed at the Treasures on the table and then swept up the cloak. He met Taliesin's eyes for a heartbeat and then swung the cloak over his shoulders.

Catrin gasped.

"Can any of you see me? Taliesin?"

"No," Taliesin said.

Cade pulled Caledfwlch from its sheath. "And now?"

"No again," Taliesin said.

"What are you thinking?" Dafydd said.

Cade almost laughed to see him looking at a spot a hand's span from Cade's eyes and a foot higher. Cade walked to the door, opened it wider, and peered out.

That got more of a response from the others. Bedwyr said, "You don't really think ..."

Cade shot Bedwyr a grin he couldn't have seen. "No time like the present!" Cade slipped out the door and into the daylight. He left the door wide so they all could see him, were he to start burning up, or be struck by lightning, or experience any of a number of events Cade deemed unlikely.

Instead, what Cade thought might be true, was. He stood still for a long moment, his neck bent forward, staring at the ground, and then spread his arms and tipped his head back to look up into the sky. A ray of sunshine pooled against the curtain wall and Cade deliberately stepped into it.

Nothing.

Restraining an urge to whistle, Cade strolled back to the hut. He slipped off the cloak and dropped it onto the table. "The mantle of Arthur will protect the King of Gwynedd, once again."

"Do you see any harm in me wearing it, Taliesin, if the need arises?" Cade said.

Taliesin gazed at the swath of fine wool. "All magic comes at a cost, but I think the price for this one has already been paid."

"As with Caledfwlch," Cade said.

Taliesin bowed his head. "As you say."

Now it really was time to go. "Taliesin, a moment," Cade said. "The rest of you—I need you to keep your eyes and ears open. I don't trust Rhys, for all that he appears to side with us now."

"Yes, sir." Dafydd had his hand at Angharad's waist in what Cade saw as a proprietary fashion, and steered her out the door towards the hall. Bedwyr saluted him as he left.

"And Goronwy," Cade said before he departed with the others, "I'll see you in the hall for the Council Meeting."

Goronwy halted in the doorway. "Why me?"

"You are the eldest of Cade's knights, the son of the King of the Isle of Man, and a leader of men in your own right," Taliesin said. "Your own father could claim the High Kingship if he chose."

Goronwy muttered under his breath and then raised his voice so they could hear him. "The question was rhetorical."

Cade smiled and shot him an amused glance. "If I have to suffer through another one of these meetings, so do you."

Goronwy grimaced and left.

Cade turned to Taliesin. "What am I to do with these?" He fingered each item in turn—the cloak, the knife, the whetstone, and the false Dyrnwyn—that remained on the table. "They can't stay here; I'm not going to stay here and who shall guard them when I'm gone? Will I have to bring them with me everywhere I go?"

"That is going to be a problem, but it is for another day," Taliesin said. "If you like, I could take one, or all, or none, as you see fit."

Cade studied his friend. "To what end? Are you leaving me again?"

"Mabon is seeking the remaining Treasures," Taliesin said. "Someone has to counter him. Your tasks are many, with what you have before you today, this week, and this year, without concerning yourself with this task too."

"Do you suggest we scatter them again to keep them from him?"

"That might be wise," Taliesin said. "But we have to think about the manner in which we do it. Whoever scattered them the first time thought they'd be safe with the families with whom he entrusted them."

"And they were," Cade said. "For a time."

"It might have even been the great King Arthur who did this, before his death," Taliesin said.

"Before we follow in his footsteps," Cade said, "we must understand how Mabon found the location of each of the Treasures in the first place." Cade picked up the knife and dropped it, frustrated as always by his lack of knowledge. He might be a *sidhe*—some of the time—but he was not on a par with the gods, no matter how powerful he might appear to his fellow men. He scoffed at his pretentions under his breath, but then a slight sound from Taliesin had him looking up.

Taliesin was gazing at him with an unreadable expression.

Cade gazed back, uncertain as to what his friend was seeing. "What's wrong?"

"You haven't mentioned gathering the Treasures for yourself," he said. "Not even once."

"Why would I want them?" Cade said. "It's Mabon who seeks that kind of power, not me. Never me."

"It would greatly enhance your ability to influence the High Council, not to mention enable you to control Mabon and whoever else opposes you in the world of the *sidhe*."

At that Cade laughed. "If that is true, I may reconsider! I would give much for that kind of power."

"And," Taliesin said, "they would help you fend off the Saxons. There is every reason to want to gather them to yourself."

"You're not seriously suggesting this? You of all people?"

Taliesin shook his head. "I'm not suggesting it as much as putting the choice out in the open. If you reject the opportunity—if you choose to gather the Treasures but not use them—you need to know what you're giving up."

"When have I ever had that kind of ambition?" Cade said. "It's a fool's quest. A man could go mad pursuing them. Perhaps Mabon already has."

"Be that as it may, are there others besides Caledfwlch you would keep, at least for now?" Taliesin said. "The items were created because they were useful, after all."

Cade spoke without hesitation. "The cloak. It uniquely serves my peculiar needs. The whetstone may help us defeat the Saxons this one time, but too many men aren't worthy of it and the men who are worthy of it are precisely the ones who don't need it. The knife is useless in battle. While I appreciate the fact that with it, I have the ability to feed my men, whole villages would benefit from it in times of famine. It would be wrong to keep it to myself." Cade glanced at his friend. "You should take that one with you on your travels."

"You know me well." Taliesin gestured to the fake Dyrnwyn. "And this sword?"

"Even if it were real, I have a sword that suits me." Cade patted his hip.

Taliesin traced the ornate designs on the sword's hilt with one finger. "I believe Dafydd is mistaken. This is the real Dyrnwyn, my lord."

Cade glanced at him, surprised both at his words and at his uncharacteristic use of Cade's title. "Really?"

"The magic of Dyrnwyn is not easily discerned," Taliesin said. "Arawn bore it and bent it to his will, but did not master it. Gofannon, the divine smith, forged it, along with the horn of immortality. The latter he gave to his sister, Arianrhod, while he gave the sword to his brother, Gwydion, the great warrior."

"Your patron," Cade said.

"Indeed."

"And why do you say this is that same sword?" Cade said. "I saw it in Arawn's possession; I held it afterwards and it flamed for me. Even Dafydd was worthy to draw it. We've both held *this* sword and it lies in our hands, limp."

"Did Dafydd hold it with the intent to use it?" Taliesin said. "Have you?"

Cade went still. "No. Neither of us." Cade gazed down at the sword and like Taliesin had done, traced the writing on the hilt and then along the blade. "Why do you say it's the real one?"

"I read the inscription: *only thou who art noble in heart may wield me.*"

"Remarkably self-explanatory, if anyone could actually read the words," Cade said.

"There are few of us left," Taliesin said.

"There's one left, you mean," Cade said, gently.

"Perhaps."

"Having found it, through considerable effort, why would Mabon leave it behind?"

"Didn't Dafydd say that Mabon appeared not to know how to wield a sword? That he sweated as he held it? Dyrnwyn does not bestow allegiance lightly. Mabon might

- 14 -

have realized that claiming this particular Treasure, at least, was a mistake."

Cade nodded, still fingering Dyrnwyn's hilt.

"Try it," Taliesin said.

Cade had told Taliesin that he wasn't tempted to keep the Treasures and that was the truth. Power as Mabon understood it was overrated, in Cade's opinion. Love was much harder to come by. But still ... Cade straightened his shoulders and picked up Dyrnwyn. He respected Taliesin's foresight, so braced himself for the possibility that he was right. He spun on one heel, slashing the blade through the air as if decapitating an unseen opponent.

The hilt warmed, and then in a flash of fire and light, blazed from hilt to tip. A storm of power filled the room and words echoed in the small chamber: *Hail Cadwaladr ap Cadwallon, King of the Britons!*

Cade dropped the sword on the table so fast he feared in retrospect that it would burn the wood. It didn't. Nor had it burned him. Still, his hands trembled. "Did you hear that?"

"I heard it," Taliesin said, "although no one else could have. The voice came from the world of the *sidhe*. What do you think Mabon might have heard when he drew it? Something, perhaps, that frightened him into abandoning it? Some say these Treasures have minds of their own."

Cade stared at Taliesin, his eyes wide. "This changes everything."

"Everything, and nothing," Taliesin said.

Without looking at his friend, because he couldn't quite bear to see the wisdom in his eyes, Cade wrapped the priceless artifacts in the cloak and tucked them under his arm.

"The Saxons will be here in two days," Cade said.

"Yes," Taliesin said.

If only Cade could have been as certain of victory.

2

Goronwy

Goronwy had taken all of a dozen breaths in the hall—or what passed for a hall since half of it was open to the air—before he found himself grinding his teeth and regretting every moment that he spent among these supposed allies.

"How do we know that you are not in league with the *sidhe* more than us?"

That was Rhys again, who seemed to feel that he had become the spokesman for all of the lords of Powys. Goronwy wished Arthur could have come, or Hywel's father, or even Angharad's. Any one of them would have been preferable to having to listen to Rhys and his father, Morgan.

But Arthur was dead and the others had felt it impossible to leave their people while Mabon—or the Saxons—were so dangerous. Hywel had led the contingent of his father's men and been proud to do it. But in the eyes of the lords here, he was a boy. Goronwy glanced at Cade—who himself was only twenty-two. Cade didn't meet his eyes. Goronwy's stomach sank into his boots: Cade needed Goronwy himself to speak.

Goronwy rose slowly to his feet. "I have something to say."

He was pleased that a palpable sense of relief wafted throughout the room. He wasn't the only one who was sick of Rhys' pronouncements and answers masquerading as questions.

"By all means." Morgan made a welcoming gesture. "The son of the King of Man has every right to speak in this company."

"I confess to being confused by this meeting," Goronwy said. "Are we here to fight the Saxons, or to fight among ourselves?"

Rhys snorted. "The Saxons, of course."

"Then what is the question at issue?" Goronwy said. "Who shall lead us? Surely that is a simple matter." He turned to Cade. "Only one man has defeated an army of Saxons in recent memory, and that is the King of Gwynedd."

Cade's teeth were clenched, but he did the right thing, which was lift his hand in acknowledgment of his achievement.

Goronwy turned back to the company. Nobody else had said anything. "If the issue at hand is the High Kingship, which so far nobody has openly spoken of, then surely that is an issue to be decided another day. If we do not defeat the Saxons here, whomever we've chosen as High King will rule over a country that doesn't exist."

"Well said." Morgan stood. "But I differ with you as to who should lead." He nodded his head at Cade. "While I admit to King Cadwaladr's recent triumphs, where are his men? I have brought far more than he and I believe that my son, Rhys, should unite our forces here."

"The men of Gwynedd are here!"

Beside Goronwy, Cade sighed as Tudur and his brother-in-law, Pod, marched into the room.

"We follow King Cadwaladr," Tudur said. "There is none whom we trust more to lead us."

"Such is the sentiment of every man here, regarding his overlord." Morgan's voice was smooth though Goronwy was sure he saw unhappiness in Morgan's face at Tudur's arrival. Wouldn't he rather have more men to fight the Saxons, even if it meant his son didn't lead the Welsh forces?

"But we must counter the Saxons," Morgan continued. "I propose a compromise. King Cadwaladr shall lead his men in battle." Morgan bowed his head towards Cade. "Rhys shall lead the men of Powys. No one shall be forced to follow someone he does not trust."

Goronwy stared at Morgan, appalled. It was like having two cooks in the kitchen. It never worked and everyone suffered from burned food.

"I do not object to such a decision," Cade said.

Goronwy glared at him, wanting to throttle his king. They both knew who was the better leader. Every man in the room knew who was the better leader. But Cade wasn't willing to create disunity at the cost of his own ascendancy and the other men didn't want to go against Morgan. Goronwy looked back at Morgan, who had a smile of satisfaction on his face. There was something wrong here, currents that Goronwy couldn't follow.

Morgan smiled. "Is that settled, then?"

* * * * *

"Christ on the cross! Why didn't you say anything?"

Goronwy and Cade stood alone on a lower rampart. Dawn was coming, and they watched the eastern plains for a sign of the Saxons. Goronwy had slept fitfully, cursing himself for how the meeting had turned out, but not knowing what he could have done to change it. In the darkness, he'd gone looking for Cade, who hadn't slept at all. That was normal for him, of course, but Goronwy thought he saw a haggard look in Cade's eyes. Sleep might have refreshed him.

Cade lowered his hands. He'd been cupping them around his eyes so he could see further. Goronwy had found that this helped him less lately than it used to.

"What would you have had me do?" Cade said. "Lose all of the men of Powys in a fit of pique? We can work with Rhys. Morgan is leaving Caer Fawr at first light, along with most of the older men on the Council. Without his father to bolster his opinion of himself, Rhys is malleable."

"You think so?" Goronwy said. "More likely, he decides he's infallible and kills us all in some stupid gambit he thinks will defeat the Saxons."

Cade turned fully to Goronwy who clenched his fists to keep his hands from shaking. So rarely did he find himself this angry, he didn't quite know what to do.

"You really think I was wrong, don't you?" Cade said. "That I should have asserted whatever authority I had to push the council towards appointing me?"

Goronwy took in a deep breath and eased it out. "I respect your judgment, my lord, more than any man's, but your greatest fault is that you don't recognize your own strengths as fully as you should."

"I would not rule men against their will." Cade pointed east, to the Saxon forces they couldn't yet see. "Not when death sits on the horizon and I'm a *sidhe*."

"I understand that this power you have is not something you've chosen," Goronwy said. "But Arianrhod gave it to you anyway. She chose you. To deny that of which you are capable is to lie to yourself. I'm not saying that your humility is false, but that it is misplaced."

Goronwy didn't like the discomfited look he saw in Cade's eyes, but he didn't look away. Someone had to tell him the truth. Even Taliesin hadn't in this instance.

"Those are strong words, Goronwy," Cade said.

"But truthful ones as I see it."

Cade rested his elbows on the turf wall of the rampart, his chin in his hands. "Yesterday, Taliesin offered me the Thirteen Treasures as a means to gather power to myself. To rule all Britain as no man as done since the days of Arthur."

"And you refused him," Goronwy said.

"Of course," Cade said.

"I don't necessarily disagree with that decision," Goronwy said. "Meddling in the affairs of the *sidhe* never results in a predictable outcome. That's not to say, however, that you shouldn't use the gifts that God has given you."

Cade scrubbed at his hair with both hands, leaving it standing on end, and then dropped them to his sides. "You are right. Of course you are right."

"I don't want to be right," Goronwy said.

"Worse, because I failed to take up the mantle of leadership here, it will be my fault if we lose men over Rhys' poor decision-making."

Goronwy swallowed hard. "I wouldn't have put it that starkly..."

"But that is what you're saying, isn't it?"

"Rhys' decisions are his own," Goronwy said. "Each man makes his own choices and his are not your fault, my lord."

"Even if I could have averted them?" Cade said. "What use is honor and nobility if somebody dies because I failed to put Rhys and Morgan in their place."

"Then again, even had the Council named you general in this battle, that's not to say Rhys or his men would have followed you. Perhaps they would have left us, as you feared," Goronwy said. And then swallowed hard, for he realized he was arguing for a position he hadn't before considered.

Cade eyed him and now it was Goronwy's turn to feel discomfited. Goronwy sighed. "Which is why you didn't force their hand. I am chastised. Forgive me, my lord."

"My lords."

Goronwy and Cade turned to see Catrin standing ten feet away with downturned lashes, having kept her distance from their conversation. It had been heated, however, and if she'd stood there any length of time, she couldn't have failed to hear what they'd said. She held a tray with food and drink for them. Despite the lingering unease at the exchange he'd just had with Cade, Goronwy was pleased that there was enough food for ten men. That meant there'd be enough for him, even if Cade ate his fill.

"Thank you, Catrin," Goronwy said.

Catrin approached and set the tray on the wall beside Goronwy. She kept her eyes towards the ground but she didn't fool Goronwy with her show of temerity.

"You heard us," he said, not as a question.

"I apologize, my lords, but I couldn't help it."

Cade glanced upwards to the rampart above them that protected the fort proper. "Did others?"

"I don't believe so, my lord," Catrin said. "It wasn't loud as all that. Besides, the men in the fort are preoccupied with the coming battle."

"And what do you think about what Goronwy had to say to me?" Cade said.

Catrin looked at Cade for the first time. "You're asking me?"

"Why not?" Cade said. "Rhiann isn't here to give me her opinion. Yours will have to suffice."

Catrin shot Goronwy a piercing look he couldn't quite interpret. "I agree with Lord Goronwy that we would be better off with you as our commander, but that does not excuse Rhys his mistakes, when he makes them. It was his choice to press so hard for the role. It is his choice to take advantage of your lack of ambition."

Goronwy studied Catrin. She'd raised her head as she'd continued speaking, no longer feigning a retiring nature— any more than that was Cade's true personality. Lord and witch exchanged long looks, before Cade nodded. "I give way," he said, "though it is too late to change the Council's decision. However, I will not allow Rhys to ruin our chances of victory out of ignorance."

"How are you going to stop him?" Goronwy said.

"I'll think of something."

"I think you have to be prepared to overrule Rhys if need be," Catrin said, looking at Cade with a steady gaze. "It might be possible to persuade him of the proper course of action, but the time might come when he refuses to listen."

"Understood," Cade said.

Catrin's shoulders relaxed. Goronwy managed to catch her eye and nodded encouragingly.

"What is the mood of the men?" Cade said. "Perhaps you have a thought on that too."

"They are ready to fight," she said. "They haven't seen the Saxon force yet, of course, so that could change."

"And that means I must speak to Taliesin." With a nod at them both, Cade strode away, back up to the fort.

Cade hadn't touched the food Catrin had brought and now there was too much. "Stay and eat with me," Goronwy said.

"I would like that." Catrin hitched herself onto the rampart beside her tray. "Angharad and I have been run off our feet in the kitchen."

Goronwy leaned against the wall. "It will get even busier up there once the fighting starts. We will need your healing skills then."

Catrin bowed her head in acceptance. "It would be an honor to assist in any way I can." She turned her head to look where Cade had gone. "He is a ruler whom a man could follow to the ends of the earth. As I understand you have."

"He's married," Goronwy said.

Catrin choked on a swallow of mead. She spit and coughed until Goronwy had to clap her on the back to loosen her throat. "I'm fine," she said—finally—laughing through her tears. "You mistake me. I have no designs on your lord."

Goronwy's eyes narrowed. "Then what?"

"You can learn much of what you need to know about a man by the lord he chooses to follow." Catrin spoke with that disconcerting frankness that had marked her from the first moment they'd met. "You, Dafydd, Taliesin ..."

As she said Taliesin's name, Catrin jumped lightly down. Then, she spun on her heel to march away, back towards the fort.

Goronwy had to smile. *Taliesin.* While Goronwy was pleased he was such a good judge of his fellow man—or woman, rather—he almost felt sorry for Taliesin. He had no idea what he was in for.

3

Rhiann

Rhiann had ridden the whole way from Dinas Bran with fear at her heels, terrified that she wouldn't reach Caer Fawr before the Saxons did. The worst thing in the world would be to watch from a distant hill as enemies slaughtered her people. Not that she could be the one to save them, but if they were going to die, perversely, she wanted to be with them. Besides, she didn't believe it was going to happen. Cade was too good a commander and his men had promised to come.

She and the three men she'd brought with her, including the garrison captain, Alun, crested the last rise before Caer Fawr and pulled up. The moon lit the sky from horizon to horizon. The mountains of Wales lay to the west but more were below, for Caer Fawr sat on a lonely hilltop, with the Severn Plain and the Breidden hills in the distance to the southeast.

Cade had told her that a spring precipitated from the peak and flowed down the hill near the west entrance to the fort. That was the one for which she and her companions would aim.

"They come." Alun pointed with one finger. Torches massed in the distance to the east. It could only be the Saxon army. She wasn't quite too late.

"But why?" Rhiann said. "Caer Fawr is impregnable. Even they should know that."

"They don't know mountains, do they?" Alun said. "Maybe they hope to starve us out."

"That doesn't sound like Penda, though, does it?" Rhiann said. "Cade has studied Penda's victories. Aggression is his trademark, although he's not been above treachery and assassination too."

Alun had fought with her father and his Saxon allies before Cadfael's death and knew what she was talking about. He barked a laugh. "Penda *is* more likely to favor a frontal assault."

It was nice to laugh, even in the face of the Saxon army. Rhiann didn't know how many men Penda had, couldn't begin to count them, but it was surely thousands. She hadn't understood the scale of what the Welsh were facing. Cade had known, if only because his own father had fought among the Saxons for so many years.

Then again, so had hers.

Rhiann and Alun gazed east, gauging the distance between Caer Fawr and the Saxon force. "They seem to be resting where they are, but I predict they'll move at first light," Alun said. "The Saxons will reach us by noon."

"We'll be ready."

Then, as they'd descended from the hills, the hundreds of men who filled the valley Caer Fawr guarded came into view. Cade might not have the thousands upon whom the Saxons could draw—but maybe he had enough. Rhiann's heart lifted.

The sun was just peaking over the eastern horizon when Rhiann and her companions made their way through the men camped to the west and behind the fort and up the hill to the hall. Most of the flags sported the crest of Madog of Powys and his son Rhys. But Tudur's flag was there, and Hywel's. Men ran back and forth from the fort to the encampment, shouting at each other.

"The Saxons! The Saxons!"

"I thought we had until noon?" Rhiann said.

Alun pursed his lips as he gazed down at the encampment. "We have some time, yet. That's just fear you're hearing."

Rhiann hoped he was right, but didn't like the idea that men were already desperate, inside the fort or out of it. Rhiann had never known Cade's men to panic.

Another shout came from the ramparts above them and Rhiann looked up to see who called to her. Bedwyr waved a hand. She returned the greeting and hurried through the gate. More men ran from hall to barracks to stables and back again.

"This way." Bedwyr helped Rhiann from her horse and took her elbow. "The sun has forced Cade to retreat inside."

Rhiann could read the tension in the set of Bedwyr's shoulders so she didn't question him as she went with him up the steps to the door, which swung open before she reached it.

Goronwy waved her inside. "He's not going to like it that you're here."

"I know," Rhiann said. "But I have news that couldn't wait."

"And you couldn't send another to deliver it?"

"I'll take chastisement from my husband, Lord Goronwy. Don't you start too!"

Goronwy surprised her with a laugh. "He's missed you. Perhaps you can put him in a better temper."

"I hope so too, but I wouldn't count on it." Rhiann passed among the dozens of men who milled about the hall until she reached a table near a caved-in dais. Cade leaned heavily on his hands, a plan of Caer Fawr and the lands around it spread before him. She hesitated, still some yards away, drinking him in. He'd pulled his nearly black hair into a leather thong at the base of his neck and wore a rich blue shirt that exactly matched his eyes.

"I'm sorry, Cade—"

Cade bent his head over the table, gripping the edges with both hands. "I heard what you said to Goronwy." Then he growled and straightened. "Come here, girl."

Rhiann went to him. Her heart had lightened at the mere thought of him. The reality was so much better. She wrapped her arms around his waist and put her face into his chest. "I missed you so much."

He lifted her arms to place them around his neck and bowed his head to touch hers. "When the lookout said you were coming, I was so angry... I didn't want you here. But now ..." He kissed her and she hung onto him for dear life.

When they drew apart, just a fraction, she said, "Mabon visited me. I didn't feel like I had any choice but to come."

"I don't want to hear this." Cade gripped her arms tightly, his tension returned, though thankfully no longer directed at her. She'd rehearsed what she was going to say to him the whole way down from Dinas Bran and she eased out a breath, glad she'd read him right. Then, he lifted his head and waved to Goronwy and Bedwyr that they should approach. "Get the others. Rhiann has brought us more bad news."

* * * * *

"So what can I do?" Rhiann said.

Angharad and Catrin looked up from their work. They were sorting through dozens of scraps of linen. It was always the one aspect of warfare that men forgot—or perhaps they didn't want to remember. Men would die in this battle but some would be wounded, and someone needed to attend them.

"I'm sure you don't need to help us, my lady," Angharad said. "The Queen of Gwynedd—"

"Hush," Rhiann said. "Don't be ridiculous. You need every hand that can be spared."

Angharad subsided and now Catrin smiled at Rhiann. "We have more than enough work to keep you occupied, my lady, if you're looking to hide from the King."

"Call me, Rhiann." Catrin's casual acceptance of her presence lifted some of Rhiann's worry. "My husband wasn't so mean as that. But I am on a short leash." Rhiann moved towards the pile of linen. Sorting it wasn't a difficult job, just necessary.

Angharad still hesitated to begin working again. "But surely, as the Queen of Gwynedd ..."

"As I reminded myself the other day before Mabon visited me, I was a serving wench long before I turned queen." Rhiann gestured to the bandages. "Many of these are dirty. We'll have to clean these before we can use them on the men."

"I asked King Cadwaladr's permission to leave the fort, to wash them in the river," Catrin said. "He was reluctant to give us leave with all these men about whom he doesn't know."

"But surely—" Rhiann thought for a moment. "The spring begins its flow just outside the western gate. There must be a spot not far from the walls where we would be safe." She held up a cloth, revealing the scrape of dirt across the middle of it.

"These aren't much use as they are," Catrin said. "But your lord won't be happy if you leave the fort."

"I'll speak to him," Rhiann said.

"He's in council with Rhys," Catrin said. "Taliesin is with him."

Rhiann thought she heard a hitch in Catrin's voice when she said Taliesin's name and made a mental note to get to know Catrin better if she could. If they had the time.

"Lord Hywel went to inventory our stock of arrows," Angharad said. "But Dafydd might be free help us."

Rhiann smiled to herself at Angharad's obvious regard for Dafydd. She was more transparent than Catrin. Still, Rhiann had only been at Caer Fawr a few hours. She didn't know if either man was aware of the interest they'd engendered. And maybe they'd never know, if the coming fight didn't go well for them.

"We'll find him," Rhiann said.

Dafydd proved amenable, so it was he and the three women who left the fort by the western gate and wended their way among the ramparts, heading steadily away from the fort. Soon they came to a rocky outcrop, from which the spring precipitated. They followed a narrow path beside it that cut through the remaining ramparts until it neared the bottom of the hill. There, a few stubby trees still grew that Cade hadn't ordered taken down. Further on, perhaps two hundred yards, Rhys' men camped.

A hillock hid the companions from the river. Before they came around it on the path, however, Rhiann pulled up short. "I hear a woman singing." She turned to the Dafydd. "We'll need to bring the camp followers inside the fort before the battle begins."

"I'll see that the word goes out," Dafydd said.

The lilting tones carried through the mid-morning air, but in words that Rhiann couldn't make out. Rhiann picked up the pace, anxious to see who it was that sang so beautifully, but Catrin grabbed her arm. "No. Don't."

"Why not?" Rhiann said.

Catrin's face had drained of all color and her eyes had gone a silver grey. Then she blinked and the impression was gone but still, Catrin held Rhiann's arm. "I can feel magic and the world of the *sidhe*," Catrin said. "It's all around us in the fort, of course, because of King Cadwaladr and the Treasures, but my sense of it had faded as we'd traversed the path, but now ..."

"Now you feel it again?" Rhiann looked ahead. The singing continued. "We must go on, if only to find out who it is."

Dafydd unsheathed his sword and stepped in front of Rhiann. "Come on."

Ten paces later, they came around the outcrop. An old woman laundered clothes on a spit of gravel in the middle of the river. She wore a gray dress and cloak and her beautiful voice was a sharp contrast to her beaked nose and scraggily hair.

Dafydd pulled up short. "It's just an old wom—"

"No it isn't!" Rhiann threw herself past him and into the channel that separated them from the old woman. She went under the surface and came up sputtering. Seeing Rhiann's mistake, Catrin raced along the grassy bank, coiled herself in preparation, and leapt across the channel. She landed on the gravel bar in the middle of the stream a dozen yards from where the woman washed.

Rhiann hauled herself out of the water, scrabbling at the rocks. She planted herself in front of the woman. "How dare you!" She snatched a shirt from the woman's grasp before turning to Dafydd and Angharad. "Help Catrin get the ones she's already washed!"

Catrin had spared herself the initial dunking, but now flung herself into the water to grasp one tunic after another before they floated downstream. Angharad and Dafydd gaped at both of them, not understanding.

"It's Arianrhod!" Rhiann said. "She's washing the tunics of the men who will die in battle this day."

That spurred them into action. Meanwhile, the crone pointed her finger at Rhiann. "You, of all people, should know better. You cannot avert your fate."

"It isn't fate!" Rhiann said. "This is your choice. Why are you doing this?" Unwanted tears leaked from her eyes and she brushed them away.

Arianrhod only cackled. "You can't save them all." She'd been watching the actions of Rhiann's friends but now turned back to Rhiann. "Would death be easier to accept if I looked like this?"

Rhiann didn't have time to take in one breath before the woman had transformed herself into the form she'd always shown to Cade, that of a beautiful woman. Then in another flash, she crouched again over the washing, a crone in tattered grey.

Not looking at her, not caring that she was openly defying the goddess, Rhiann gathered the tunics from the basket that the Arianrhod still had left to wash. "You would have every one of these men dead? Why? They are your people! Why not hamper the Saxons instead of us?"

Arianrhod laughed. The tinkle of it was in sharp contrast to her earlier cackle. "I would not deprive your husband of his fight, my dear." She had returned to the shape of a beautiful woman.

Rhiann shivered. She couldn't bear to look at Arianrhod and clutched the twenty tunics she'd gathered. She was just reaching for the last item in Arianrhod's basket, when the goddess laughed again. Against her will, Rhiann's chin came up so she had to look at her. "I am the goddess of the cauldron, of war and battle, of the silver wheel of life and death." Arianrhod gazed at Rhiann and it was as if Rhiann's breath froze in her chest. "And life is what you care about, isn't it?"

The chatter of Catrin, Angharad, and Dafydd, gathering the tunics that Arianrhod had already committed to the depths, came muffled to her ears, as if she and Arianrhod stood in a crypt by themselves. Outside sounds echoed without penetrating the rock.

"Wha-what are you saying?"

Arianrhod's face was wreathed in light. She pointed to the tunics Rhiann held. "Would you trade just one of those, not your husband's of course, but Dafydd's perhaps, or Bedwyr's? Just one, for the chance to bear a son for Cade?"

Rhiann tried to swallow, but her tongue stuck to the roof of her mouth. "You ask me to exchange a friend's life for … a baby?"

"For Cadwaladr's child." Arianrhod spoke the words as if they were nothing, as if she was asking Rhiann to pass the butter.

"No." Rhiann found her head shaking back and forth, back and forth. "You can't ask that, you can't offer me that."

"But I just have." Arianrhod took a step towards Rhiann. "No one would know. We would keep it between us." She leaned closer and lowered her voice. "Just close your eyes and choose."

"No!" Rhiann threw out her arm in a gesture of denial and backed away, but the stones behind her tripped her up and she fell among them, half in and half out of the water.

Arianrhod stood over her, smiling though the smile didn't reach her eyes, even in the *glamour* she had donned.

"So be it," Arianrhod said. "Perhaps you are worthy of *him* after all."

Rhiann gaped at the goddess, who smiled serenely back.

"Rhiann!" Dafydd raced towards them.

Arianrhod shimmered, glanced back once at Dafydd, and then seemed to melt into nothingness. As Dafydd reached her, Rhiann looked around, feeling like she'd just woken up from a dream. Her hands were empty, too. Everything Arianrhod had brought to the river—the tunics, the basket, the scrubbing brush—were gone. Instead, an arrow lay among the rocks where Arianrhod had been standing. At least a yard in length, the wood was silver-grey, like the crone's dress, but with black feathers and tipped in silver.

Rhiann crawled towards it but didn't pick it up. Catrin crouched beside her and they studied the arrow together.

"Is it safe?" Rhiann said.

"A gift from the goddess is never safe," Catrin said.

Rhiann reached out a finger to touch it. As with the chess piece that Mabon had left her, when no lightning struck her, she picked it up.

"Where did Arianrhod go?" Dafydd said.

"There." Catrin pointed to the channel on the far side of the gravel bar. The goddess had assumed the shape of the crone again, solid and ugly as she trudged through the river. Her dress was soaked to her waist, but her hands were empty. She disappeared into the woods on the other side.

4

Dafydd

Rhiann was shaking so hard Dafydd was afraid she would fall out of his arms. He clutched her more tightly. Catrin and he had supported her through the water and up the bank, but she was trembling so hard she couldn't walk. Not long ago, he would have been thrilled at the thought of holding Rhiann so close, even if she was in peril, but now, all he wanted was to find Cade and pass her off. But Cade couldn't walk in the sun. Dafydd checked the sky. It would have to be someone else and he hoped he would come soon.

"Angharad—do you have the arrow?" he said, over his shoulder.

"Yes, my lord," she said.

He tsked through his teeth. She'd taken to calling him 'my lord' in the last few days and he couldn't seem to get her to stop. "Give it to Catrin and run ahead. The path is too steep and too far. I won't make it."

And that was another thing he would have been loath to admit two months ago. But a man was not measured by whether or not he could carry his queen a hundred yards straight up a mountain. Another few feet and a watcher finally spotted them. Dafydd's legs had started to tremble with the effort, and then Bedwyr arrived to rescue him.

His jaw set and grim, Bedwyr took Rhiann from Dafydd and strode away. Goronwy had come too. He took the arrow from Angharad and then escorted Catrin, still carrying their dirty cloths, the rest of the way to the fort. They'd never gotten the linen washed, but Dafydd didn't think they wanted to go back to the river to finish the job. They did have Caledfwlch after all. The sword would heal anyone who would accept Cade's help. It was just that there would be men who needed to be kept alive until Cade could help them.

Dafydd bent forward, his hands on his knees. All he could see of Angharad was her boots and the hem of her skirt. Like him, she was soaked to the waist.

"I don't understand any of what just happened," Angharad said. "Who was that woman? And what kind of hold did she have on Queen Rhiannon?"

Dafydd straightened and took in a deep breath. "You know that King Cadwaladr is a *sidhe*?"

"Yes, of course."

"Arianrhod—the goddess of time and fate, and of war—made him what he is. She has been known to visit, especially recently."

"And that's who the crone was at the river?" Angharad said. "I thought Arianrhod was a beautiful woman."

Dafydd shrugged. "She takes many forms. Legend says that before a battle, Arianrhod washes the tunics of men doomed to die in that battle." Dafydd looked at his hands, empty now of any proof of what they'd seen and done.

"I couldn't get them all," Angharad said. "Some floated away in the faster currents."

"I know," Dafydd said. "I didn't want to look but I couldn't help it. Many of them bore the crest of the boar."

"Rhys' men?"

Dafydd bit his lip. "Goronwy and I wear the eagle badge, when we don't wear Cade's red dragon. Did you see—" He broke off, realizing that he didn't want to know the answer, but Angharad was looking at him steadily.

"The crone had one such tunic with her and Rhiann tore it from her hands."

Dafydd swallowed again. This magic, this world of the *sidhe,* was not a world that he wanted anything to do with. The moment of a man's death should be a mystery, or at the very least, not determined by the opaque reasoning or whims of a feckless goddess. The moment the thought formed in his head, he struggled to suppress it. Who knew if the goddess could read his thoughts? Dafydd hoped not.

Angharad looked over the ramparts towards the stream. "Arianrhod didn't have to wash the tunics here."

"What do you mean?" Dafydd said.

"Of all the rivers in Powys to wash them in, she chose this one? Perhaps she wanted Rhiann to find her."

"I'd like you to be right," he said. "I'd like to think the goddess is on our side, at least a little bit."

Angharad turned back to him. "The news is worse than this, though."

Dafydd snorted a laugh. "How could it be worse?" And then he sobered because he realized she was serious.

"When we were coming up from the river, I overheard some of the men who passed us going the other way. Rhys has ordered his men to move out within the hour. They will meet the Saxons in the fields below Caer Fawr."

Dafydd stared at her. "He can't be serious." Dafydd looked east. "They outnumber us. To meet them in open battle loses all advantage of the high ground. That's why King Cadwaladr chose to gather his troops at Caer Fawr in the first place!"

"Rhys is preparing to march. With all of his men and ours."

Dafydd caught Angharad's arm. "You must leave. Now. Go with Catrin and Rhiann and head directly west. You have enough of a head start that they won't catch you."

Angharad tried to wrench her arm away. "I will not! You need us. I won't leave you."

Something shifted in Dafydd just then. Maybe it was her adamancy. Maybe it was her upturned nose and the freckles scattered across it that Lilwen had tried so desperately to hide. She wasn't Rhiann, but maybe she didn't have to be. He wasn't Cade either. Without thinking about it, before the impulse deserted him, Dafydd caught Angharad's hand. She looked down at their interlocked fingers and then back up at him.

"I don't want anything to happen to you," he said.

"I don't either," she said. "But how would leaving here help? The entire world is dangerous. Besides, Mabon knows that I last had the cloak. I'd be more vulnerable out there than in here."

The sound of drums and marching feet were evident as the men in the camp below them fell into lines on Rhys' orders.

"I hate to admit it," Dafydd said, "but you may be right."

5

Rhiann

"**A**nd your honor says that you must fight alongside Rhys?"

Rhiann asked the question from a curled position on the pallet that was all that adorned their chamber. King and Queen of Gwynedd they might be, but they had no more in the way of luxuries than anyone else, barring the privacy of a room.

"He is determined to face the Saxons on what he calls *his own terms*," Cade said. "I think he's trying to prove to his father that he can lead."

"He seeks to upstage you."

"When all it does is show him a fool and endanger all of us." Cade scrubbed at his hair with both hands and turned to look at his wife. That Arianrhod had appeared to her was terrifying. He'd found himself more angry—at the goddess, and the fates—than he'd ever been in his life. And he'd taken out some of that anger on Rhiann, to his regret. "I am bound—"

"You are not." Rhiann's words came out sharp and taut. "You swore no allegiance to Rhys or Morgan. You agreed to share command at Caer Fawr. That is all."

"A fine point—"

"Don't make me hurt you, Cadwaladr ap Cadwallon!" Rhiann picked up the pillow on which her head had been lying and threw it at him.

Cade caught it and then moved to her side. He knelt to wrap his arms around her. "You could never do that."

"I could," Rhiann said.

Cade looked into her eyes and his heart twisted to see tears starting in them again.

"Arianrhod wanted me to hurt you," she said.

"Something about the tunics?" he said. "I still don't understand what happened down at the river. It doesn't make sense."

"She spoke to me, Cade," Rhiann said. "I didn't want to tell you in front of all the others, but Arianrhod spoke directly to me."

His eyes narrowed. "And what did she say?"

"She offered me a bargain." Rhiann had her face pressed into his arm, refusing to look at him. Cade had never seen her like this before.

"What kind of bargain?" Cade felt his temper rising again at the idea. It was one thing for Arianrhod to speak to him, to demand his services. It was quite another for her to upset his wife.

"She offered to trade the life of one of your men, one of our friends, for a child. Our child."

Cade took in a deep breath and then swallowed down the first three things that came to his mind. He studied his wife's downturned head and then stroked back a lock of her hair that had come loose and tucked it behind her ear. Only after he'd gained some measure of control, did he speak. "And she actually thought you'd make such a bargain with her?"

Rhiann clutched his hand. "She pressed on me. Her eyes bored into me. I wanted to accept so badly, but ..."

Cade tugged on Rhiann's braid. He heard and accepted the pain in her voice. But that Rhiann would choose such a thing wasn't possible. Arianrhod should have known that. "Is a child so important, Rhiann? We've been married only a few weeks. We've not even discussed it other than in passing."

"It doesn't matter how long we're married, Cade." Rhiann finally looked into his face. "We will never have a child. You know that."

"I know it," Cade said. "But I didn't realize how much you were thinking of it already."

"Soon, everyone will begin to look askance at me," Rhiann said. "They will wonder when I will give you a son, and when I prove incapable of it, they will say that it's my fault. They'll question your decision to marry me. They'll wonder what it will take to convince you to put me aside. For the sake of Wales."

"They would be fools to think or say it," Cade said, "but I grant that biddies in the solar are often fools." He rubbed the back of her hand with his thumb. "This war has left many children fatherless. Motherless too. And there will be more after today. We could bring such a child into our house, if you like?"

Rhiann lifted her head. "Do you mean it?"

"Of course," he said. "Wasn't I mothered and fathered well by people who weren't my birth parents? Wasn't I loved as much as Rhun?"

Rhiann sat up and threw her arms around Cade's neck. She hung on, holding him tightly. "Yes. You were. And we could do the same."

* * * * *

Which was all very well and good, and Cade was delighted that Rhiann was happy, but meanwhile, they had Saxons to fight. Disaster loomed on the horizon. He left Rhiann asleep and entered the great hall. And stopped short. Hywel—alone among all his men—had chosen to confront Rhys. Cade hesitated on the threshold, wondering if he should interfere, but then thought better of it. Hywel was Rhys' brother-in-law. He had a right to speak his mind.

Hywel held Rhys' arm in a tight grip, even as Rhys tried to twist away. "You can't order your men into the field. It is suicide."

"It is the only way to show them that we are not afraid." Rhys' face showed defiance. He was either sure of himself, or wanted to be sure and was using bravado to appear so. Cade moved silently along one wall until he came abreast of the pair.

"You fought for the right to command the forces here," Hywel said, "and your first move is one that everyone counsels against? Where's the sense in that?"

"I do what I think is right," Rhys said. "As does your lord, does he not?"

Cade had come to rest just within Rhys' line of sight and Rhys' eyes flicked to him and then away. Cade, for his part, kept his face impassive. He'd already had this conversation with Rhys. Cade's choice, now, was to allow Rhys and his men to die unsupported, or to die alongside them.

"This is how you treat a member of your family?" Rhys said, deflecting the issue. "No wonder your father hasn't spoken a civil word to you in two years."

"We've spoken," Hywel said. "How did you think I arrived with a hundred of my father's men?"

"I would hope you'd be thinking of your sister," Rhys said. "Of what you owe her—and by extension, me, as your brother-in-law."

"I *am* thinking of my sister when I stand on the battlements of this keep and see five thousand Saxon soldiers within two hours' walk of this fortress!" Hywel said. "I am thinking of her when I tell you that she will be ashamed to discover that her husband allowed so many men to die for no reason! We can devise a plan to defeat them, but it won't be with on a field in front of Caer Fawr, out of arrow range of the fortress and with too few cavalry to make a difference."

"You are wrong," Rhys said. "We march now." He wrenched his arm away from Hywel's grip. Hywel's fists clenched at his sides and Cade thought he would strike Rhys, but Taliesin moved in and caught Hywel's arm, stepping between the two men and blocking Rhys' view of Hywel with his body.

"Let him go," Taliesin said. Although he lowered his voice for the next words, Cade read his lips. "Death is not the only possible future for us. We can win despite Rhys' idiocy."

Hywel stepped back. "You mean this, truly?"

Taliesin nodded. Meanwhile, Rhys glared at Taliesin's back, spun on his heel, and marched down the hall to the double doors at the far end. He waved a hand at the half dozen retainers who'd watched the scene with considerable interest. "We go! Who rides with me?"

Before Rhys' men pulled open the doors, Cade was there. Rhys hadn't seen Cade coming, but then, Cade could move quickly when he wanted to. "And what is the role you have for me?" Cade said. "I cannot ride with you. I cannot fight while the sun shines."

Rhys sneered at Cade and it was so reminiscent of the look that Mabon's face usually held that Cade faltered. Was there more to this show of force than bravado, or a son's desire to prove himself worthy of his father?

"Then you can watch our victory from the safety of the guardhouse," Rhys said.

"And if you are wrong, what then?" Cade said. "You leave us to defend Caer Fawr against a great Saxon force that will surround us. At our defeat, they will run free through Wales, picking off our castles and our lands one by one. Including your father's." Cade jerked his chin at Hywel. "Sir Hywel is right. As I predicted, Penda won't be able to resist a frontal assault. If we stay inside Caer Fawr, the Saxons will come to us. We will have the high ground, and the archers to counter any who come against us."

Rhys's teeth clenched. He gripped Cade's shoulder and for the first time, met his eyes. "We can't win from inside Caer Fawr, no matter how many men we have."

Cade's eyes narrowed at him. "Why do you say that?"

"You are not the only one whom the gods have favored with a visit," Rhys said.

"What are you saying? Who of the gods came to see you?"

"I have found favor where you have not. I am assured a victory."

Cade's mouth tasted of acid. "I'm very glad to hear it. Tell me who it was. Surely not … Mabon?"

The smirk was back and Cade considered wiping it off Rhys' face with his fist.

"The gods ally with these Saxons, but against *you*, not me, and not my men." Rhys pushed past him and into the sunlight of high noon. Cade stayed where he was. Safe but impotent.

Hywel came to stand beside him. "As I see it, we have three choices: you could kill him now, though his men might riot and we'd be no closer to victory than before, we could stay safe inside the fort and let him and his men die, or we could fight alongside them and pray for a miracle."

Cade turned his head to meet Hywel's eyes.

Hywel nodded. "You'll need the cloak."

Cade tensed his shoulders and then released it. "For all I am *sidhe*, I am only one man. This is going to be a slaughter."

6

Goronwy

"Help me!"

"God damn it!"

"That's my leg, you piece of dung!"

The words of the men around him clung to Goronwy's ear as he hacked away at the Saxon force. It was no good, of course, had been no good almost from the start, and he was hoping to God that soon Rhys would see it. If he still lived, that is.

Cade was somewhere off to his right, Bedwyr to his left. Thankfully, Cade had insisted that Hwyel, Rhiann, and Dafydd stay on the rampart with their bows. When it came to the retreat, they could defend it with their arrows.

"Fall back!"

Goronwy didn't have to be told twice. He swung his horse around and made for the gate that cut through the northern rampart. Just ahead, a foot soldier was struggling to help a friend who'd lost the use of one of his legs. Goronwy leaned down to collar the foot soldier, while Bedwyr grabbed the wounded friend by the arm and hauled him up behind him.

"Praise God! I thought we were goners." Goronwy's rescued pikeman clutched him around the waist.

Goronwy grunted at that, for he'd thought so too—about a dozen times in the last hour. He leaned over his horse's neck, averting his eyes from the setting sun. Darkness couldn't come too soon for Goronwy.

"Rhys is dead," the man said. "I saw him fall."

And for that, Goronwy had no answer. He risked a look back. Behind him, the bulk of their men had taken to their heels and were running full out for Caer Fawr.

"Why don't the Saxons follow?" Bedwyr said, also looking over his shoulder.

And then Goronwy saw why. The Saxons hadn't brought cavalry to the fight—Penda's men never fought on horseback—and that gave the single horseman who raced his horse between the Welsh retreat and the Saxons advance a tremendous advantage. Especially because that horseman was the King of Gwynedd. Although Goronwy couldn't see Cade due to the cloak, he knew he was there by the glow the cloak couldn't suppress, even in the brightness of the late afternoon sun. Cade blazed between their fleeing men and the bulk of the Saxon lines and his invisible sword cut down every Saxon who attempted to follow them.

Goronwy reached the stream that ran between the rampart and the battlefield and pulled up short. Taliesin shouted at Bedwyr while stabbing a finger in Cade's direction. "Get that fool back here right now! We need him!"

Bedwyr shoved the soldier he'd rescued off his horse and was away again, back the way they'd come. He cut through the lines of retreating men, who opened a path for him through their ranks. Fewer than half of those who'd gone out were returning.

Meanwhile, Taliesin, Dafydd, and Hywel were working furiously with sticks and rope among the trees on the near side of the stream.

Goronwy allowed the pikeman to drop to the ground and dismounted himself. He handed the reins to the young man. "Care for him with your life. This was King Arthur's horse."

The man sketched a bow. "My life belongs to you as it is." And with an insouciant grin, which told Goronwy how pleased he was to be alive, he was off.

"What are you doing?" Goronwy said to Taliesin.

"Creating a surprise for the Saxons, should they decide to continue the assault." Taliesin threw a glance at Goronwy over his shoulder. "We could use the help."

Which is how Goronwy found himself suddenly changed from knight to serf as Taliesin ordered them all about during the time it took for the last of the able-bodied men to reach the gatehouse.

"You've never shown us this type of magic before," Goronwy said.

Taliesin glanced up from his work and then back to the series of complicated knots he was tying. "We've never needed it quite this much before." Goronwy didn't know about that, and was about to say so, when Taliesin added, "Anyone who uses magic pays a price. It wouldn't do for me to use it unless in absolute need, nor for any of you to come to rely on it." One more glance. "And I'm stronger now than I was."

Last of all, Cade and Bedwyr came flying across the field towards them.

Cade reined in under the darkness of the trees and removed his cloak so they could see him. He stood in the stirrups to look east. "The Saxons will come. I'm sure of it. But we have a little time." He lifted his chin to indicate the complex weaves of ropes that Taliesin had painstakingly crafted and his friends had interspersed among the trees. "What's this?"

"When the Saxons come, you will see." Taliesin looked up at Cade. "You fought well. You saved many men."

"It helped that the Saxons have no demons among them this time," Cade said. "It leaves me with a prickling at the back of my neck. Perhaps Mabon is waiting for his chance to hound me the moment I put my guard down."

"We'll just have to do our best until then." Taliesin said this absently, his tongue peeking between his teeth as he concentrated on the task he'd set himself.

"How can you—" Cade bit off the words and looked away, back across the fields littered with Welsh fallen. Crows and birds of prey gathered above them, spiraling down in ever smaller circles to come to land. "We can't even bury our dead."

"We have a war to fight," Taliesin said. "It's time to get on with it."

Dafydd moved closer. "The men who can count have done so and come up with long odds."

"I know," Cade said. "We've had long odds before."

"But not under these circumstances," Goronwy said.

"We have enough food to last us, what with the knife," Cade said. "We can survive on half-rations for a long time."

"To what end?" Dafydd said. "We hold out until the Saxons give up or falter from illness? How long will that take? And how long, then, are we penned in here like sheep in a stockade while other armies lay waste to our lands?"

"We still haven't heard from Rhun and Siawn," Goronwy said. "They will come."

"If they can," Cade said. "Another army just like this one could be marching out of Chester as we speak. The northern barons have had their hands full too, in recent months."

Taliesin shook his head. "This is useless wondering and unlike you—all of you." The bard checked the sky. "They'll come as the sun sets. We have an hour, maybe two. Let's use it. We all have work to do."

And that was that.

"I'll save any wounded man I can." Cade turned his horse's head and trotted back towards the field, draping the cloak around himself and disappearing just before he hit the sunlight beyond the trees.

"Why are you so calm?" Goronwy said to Taliesin. None of them had mentioned the despair and rage that Goronwy had been feeling ever since he learned the size of the Saxon force and that Rhys intended to march against them.

"And what would I gain by despair?" Taliesin said.

"Did you know this would happen?" Goronwy said.

The bard stopped working. "My gift is neither clear nor certain," Taliesin said. "I see a host of possible futures. Sometimes that is almost worse than seeing none at all." He shrugged. "Almost. Every choice made both reduces and expands the possible futures. It's when they narrow to only one that I begin to worry."

"And have they? The paths you see?" Goronwy said.

Taliesin studied him. "Not yet."

"So you don't know what will happen?" Gorowny said.

With a slight shake of his head, Taliesin went back to his weaving of rope. "Only what could."

7

Hywel

Hywel glared over the ramparts at the oncoming force and barked a laugh. It was too late for second guessing. "A few hundred men from Gwynedd against a host of Saxons we've barely stung."

"But it's the same men we had when we fought the demons outside Caer Dathyl," Dafydd said.

Hywel fingered the arrows in his quiver. "Yet this time, we fight against a far greater, and less stupid, opposition." And with too few arrows. They always had too few.

"What's the accounting?" Bedwyr stepped up to the rampart to look with them. Soon the sun would set behind the hills, falling into the sea they couldn't see from where they stood. The last rays shone in the Saxons' eyes. Cade would give the order to fire the moment the Saxons came within arrow range.

Hywel gestured to one of the baskets of arrows under the rampart. "Some two thousand of them. It will still be hand to hand, far sooner than I'd like."

"At least the Saxons don't have archers," Bedwyr said.

"Or not many," Hywel said. "They hunt with bows; they just don't fight with them."

"Nor horses," Bedwyr said.

"Our advantage," Hywel said.

"Not our only one," Bedwyr said. "We have the high ground."

Hywel turned to Bedwyr, trusting him more than he had ever trusted any man, barring his father and King Cadwaladr at times. "Were we fools to follow the king? We could have left. Lived to fight another day."

"And what of Rhys and his men?" Bedwyr said. "Should we have left them to fight unsupported?"

"Either way, the Saxons will be free to pillage our lands, kill our people, without any check," Hywel said. "Penda will now happily pick the other kings off one by one."

"You assume we are going to lose," Dafydd said. "King Cadwaladr doesn't think so."

"Doesn't he?" Bedwyr said. "Or is he putting on a brave face?"

Hywel stared again at the Saxon force. Caer Fawr was protected by a system of ramparts. Two ran on each side of the fort (eastern and western) and as many as six on the southern and northern sides where the gates lay. Hywel and his friends stood on the rampart that formed the defenses for the lowest level, but was still a twenty-foot-high wall of mounded earth, with a ditch on the other side that meant the Saxons would have trouble no matter how they tried to go over it. This was where the first attack would come. Here and at the north-eastern gate.

Below him further, Cade was marshalling an initial force of archers and swordsmen at the extension to the fort that looked southeast. The Saxons had to know that the Welsh numbers were reduced. Hywel hoped that they didn't know how far.

Hywel turned around to find that Bedwyr was gone, replaced by Taliesin who was looking at him gravely. "What, no bit of poetry to mark the occasion?" Hywel said.

"Is it necessary? Because I could find an appropriate word if you needed it."

Hywel coughed on a laugh. "No."

"I meant what I said in there," Taliesin said.

Hywel sobered. "Am I going to die? Is that why you're here?"

"We are going to live, whether in fact or memory," Taliesin said. "I don't look ahead that way with my gift. But I do have a task for you, one that is dangerous, but one I feel you are uniquely suited to."

"What is it?" Hywel said. "And does it mean I'll miss your fireworks?"

Taliesin gave him a small smile. "King Cadwaladr asks that you enter the Saxon camp to speak to Penda."

Hywel stared at him. "What? Why? To what end? Penda smells blood. He won't back off."

"He might reconsider, if he knew what I know."

"And King Cadwaladr wants me to deliver this message—one that Penda is sure not to like?" Hywel said.

"He needs someone who speaks Saxon, as you do, and is smart enough to get in without being seen and out without dying," Taliesin said.

Hywel licked his lips. "King Cadwaladr knows I speak Saxon? Does he also know—" Hywel broke off, reluctant to finish the sentence.

"That your father is also Saxon? That he was one of Penda's staunch allies until the killing sickened him to the point that he fled for Wales? You forget that Cadwaladr's own mother is Penda's sister. There is little he doesn't know."

"If Penda discovers who I really am ..."

"He might kill you," Taliesin said.

"You've seen it?"

"It is one possible future, but I don't think it likely."

Hywel bit off a comment about how that was all well and good for Taliesin, but it was *his*—Hywel's—life they were talking about. "That's a relief."

"I suggest you don't tell him,"

"What *am* I to tell him?"

"What I have *seen*."

"And that is?" Hywel said. It was like pulling teeth to get Taliesin to give him any solid piece of information. He could be so infuriating at times, as if everyone else could *see* too and he only had to allude to some future event and everyone would understand. Either that or he enjoyed the suspense. Hywel suspected that was just as likely.

"That Oswin of Northumbria has gathered an army on the northern border of Mercia. If Penda takes the time to fight here and loses many men, he won't have a country left to defend or enough men to defend it, even if he defeats us."

"King Cadwaladr thinks he might withdraw?" Hope sparked in Hywel's chest, which he instantly suppressed. Penda would never withdraw. He would look a coward.

"No," Taliesin said. "But he might think better of a fight to the death. He might see a thousand men fall to our arrows and believe that what I saw was true."

"And is it true, in fact?"

"True enough," Taliesin said.

Whatever that meant.

8

Dafydd

"You're letting her fight?" Dafydd forced himself to back away rather than get right in Cade's face as he wanted. Cade's office was so small, there wasn't much room as it was. Dafydd clenched his fists. "Are you out of your mind?"

"She is not your wife, Dafydd," Cade said. "This is not your decision."

"I fought with her in Llangollen and at Caer Dathyl," Dafydd said. "I know better than you of what she is capable and I don't want her put at risk again. She shouldn't even be here!"

"I couldn't agree more," Cade said. "But she is here. Are you telling me you don't need another bow?"

"Of course we do—but not hers! She should stay with Angharad and Catrin among the wounded."

"What's gotten into you, Dafydd? You've never objected to her fighting before." Cade folded his arms across his chest. Dafydd had been in love with Rhiann, he knew, but his behavior towards Angharad had seemed proprietary. *What am I missing?*

"What's gotten into me?" Dafydd paced around the small room. "Why are women here at all? They've no business on the battlefield, even if we have twenty-foot walls surrounding us. We should have sent them away while we had the chance. *You* should have sent them away."

"And where would they go? Rhiann is the wife of the King of Gwynedd. Penda has already tried to corral her once and marry her to Peada. Do you think any place in Wales will be safe for her if I fall?"

"What if the Saxons break through? How safe will our hall be then?"

"They won't—"

"Damn right, they won't!" Dafydd said.

"Ah," Cade said.

Dafydd glared at him, not liking the sudden knowing tone. "What?"

"You think this is your fault, don't you?" Cade said. "It was you who brought Angharad here, and now you are afraid for a woman like you've never been afraid before."

Dafydd stopped his pacing, glared at Cade, and strode from the room, slamming the door behind him. Cade barked a laugh through the door but Dafydd kept going. He crossed the great hall at a trot, determined to get outside as quickly as possible. He didn't want to talk about his disagreement with his king, and particularly not the role Angharad had played in it. As far as Dafydd was concerned, King Cadwaladr saw far too much. If Dafydd had thought Rhiann was willful, she had nothing on Angharad. *I sure can pick them...*

Leave it to Angharad, however, to notice his flushed face and move to intercept him. He slowed and forced a calmer expression. But when she came abreast, she had something else on her mind. "Taliesin wants you on the ramparts."

He glanced at her. "Why?"

"They're coming. Now."

Dafydd picked up the pace. "I just left the King. Does he know?"

"Rhiann went to tell him."

"So why does Taliesin want me?" Dafydd said.

"Something about you needing to shoot an arrow to start it off," Angharad said.

Dafydd didn't know what that meant, but he didn't argue, just hurried across the courtyard and through the gate to the spot on the rampart where Taliesin waited, looking east at the oncoming Saxons. As it turned out, it wasn't the main force after all, but a party on horseback, perhaps looking to probe the Welsh defenses.

"What do they think they're doing?" Dafydd said. "They'll be within arrow range in a moment."

"I've asked Cadwaladr to let them come," Taliesin said.

"How close?" Dafydd said.

"You know exactly how close. You helped me set the traps." Taliesin eyebrows practically met in a look that told Dafydd he thought Dafydd was an idiot but was too polite to say so.

"Rope and sticks were all I saw," Dafydd said.

"Well, you'll see more in a moment," Taliesin said. "I'll need you to shoot an arrow, one of my own design, exactly where I tell you to. We don't have much time before it's full dark."

Dafydd gripped his bow, hoping Taliesin's trust wasn't misplaced. Angharad and Catrin hovered on the margins of their conversation. Taliesin looked over and waved them nearer. "There's nothing to fear. At least, not for you up here."

"I can feel your magic," Catrin said. "It's rising."

For the first time ever, Taliesin actually looked discomfited and then his expression smoothed. "As it should be. You might be a better judge even than I am of when I should release it."

Catrin surprised Dafydd by nodding her agreement. He wasn't sure how he felt about having both Catrin and Taliesin next to him. There were undercurrents here he'd last felt only in Arawn's cavern.

The Saxon cavalry neared the line of bushes that followed the little river. Dafydd split his attention between them and Taliesin who brought out a three-foot long, slender stick and held it out across his palm. He muttered words Dafydd didn't catch in a language he didn't understand. Dafydd found himself growing dizzy watching him, as if the stick were wavering between the world of magic and his own.

"Dafydd!" Catrin caught his bow arm and he jerked back to himself to find Taliesin gazing at him, a smile twitching at his lips. The stick had become an arrow with a golden point, which he handed to Dafydd.

"Press it into the bow," Taliesin said.

Dafydd didn't ask him to say *please*. He fitted the arrow to his bow and pressed into it. Then Taliesin, his staff in his left hand and his right hand outstretched, pointed his index finger at the tip of the arrow and uttered a soundless incantation. It lit with a purple fire.

The ropes they'd positioned at Taliesin's direction also glowed purple and Taliesin pointed at a spot on the ground on the far side of the creek. "There!"

Dafydd loosed the arrow. It flew through the air and hit—

Whuf!

The bushes exploded and the concussion that followed had Dafydd on his knees with his hands over his ears. Angharad fell into him as the wave of power passed over them. With his arm around her, Dafydd staggered to his feet.

The magic had torn the earth on the far side of the creek asunder, the trees and scrub that had lined it were in flames, and all but three of the two dozen Saxon cavalry were down. The remainder raced towards the Saxon lines.

Cade ran down the path between the ramparts, his eyes wide. "What was that, Taliesin? You said you had a surprise for them but ..."

Taliesin's eyes were bright. "That went better than I expected. I'd only done a small trial earlier to see if it worked. If I'd known it would go so well, I would have saved it for when the bulk of the army marched on us."

"You could do it agai—" But Dafydd cut off his words at the sudden whiteness in Taliesin's face. The bard staggered and would have gone down if Cade hadn't caught him.

"Power has a price," Catrin said.

Cade bent and threw Taliesin over his shoulder. "Warn me next time, will you, Taliesin? You're the king of understatement." Cade strode back to the keep with Taliesin on his shoulder.

Dafydd would have laughed if Taliesin didn't look so ill.

Angharad slipped her hand into his and they turned back to the devastation below them. "Here's hoping the price he pays is worth it," she said.

9

Hywel

Hywel crouched in the trees. Darkness had fallen, made even thicker by the heavy cloud cover that had blown in with it. The first raindrops fell. Above him on the hill, his own men shouted to each other about Taliesin's handiwork, while the Saxons gathered two hundred yards away. That they were Saxon and not demon, he had no doubt. He didn't know where Mabon was in all this, and by now he didn't much care. He had a job to do.

"Thought you'd try this without me, did you?" Bedwyr's gruff voice sounded in Hywel's ear. He didn't bother turning to look at his friend, since he couldn't see anything anyway.

"King Cadwaladr sent only me," Hywel said. "This isn't your task."

"Ach," Bedwyr said and Hywel felt the accompanying shrug. "I told him he was an idiot for letting you go alone."

Now Hywel did turn, searching for Bedwyr's face in the murk. "And what did the King say?"

Bedwyr guffawed—quietly. "He laughed. He knew I was right. I told him that I couldn't let you die before you'd found a girl to come home to."

Hywel scoffed. "Like Dafydd? He's taken to Angharad pretty quick."

"They rode north together for two days. It doesn't take long. Besides ..." Bedwyr peered over Hywel's shoulder. "This is what I do best."

And that, Hywel decided, was probably true. Bedwyr hadn't been raised in a castle, nor to the sword, though he fought as well as any of the other knights. He'd fallen in with Goronwy not long after Goronwy's arrival in Gwynedd. They'd fought together ever since and when Goronwy had learned of Cade's existence, Bedwyr hadn't considered letting him join Cade's *teulu* without him.

"Then let's do it," Hywel said.

At a crouch, the two men raced forward, skirting the Saxon lines to the west and staying within the trees that lined the little river that separated Caer Fawr from the rest of the valley it overlooked—and that Taliesin had so effectively destroyed.

They peered at the camp from underneath a bush. A steady drip of water fell on both of them and Hywel's front was already muddy to his chin. In the time it had taken them to reach this point, the Saxons seemed to have gotten themselves together again. The explosion had been a shock, but they'd lost fewer than two dozen men. They'd be more cautious from now on than they would have been, but it looked like they hadn't changed their minds about their attack.

Maybe Hywel could help Penda with that.

"We've barely dented their numbers, Bedwyr said.

"Rhys was a fool," Hywel said.

"He's in the Otherworld now," Bedwyr said. "He can tell Arawn all about his defeat and how he ignored Cade's best judgment. And got so many good men killed."

Hywel suddenly had a cold feeling in his belly. "Arawn isn't powerless, you know, for all that Gwyn guards the cauldron and will not let him out. He roams freely in the world of the *sidhe*."

"So?"

"What if Rhys speaks to him of our efforts here? What if he tells Mabon where we are?"

"Didn't you hear what Rhys told Cade?" Bedwyr said. "Mabon came to Rhys already and assured him of victory."

"Lied to him, you mean." Hywel shook his head—and then shook off his worries, glad his tasks were more grounded than Cade's. Hywel agreed with Dafydd: he'd had enough of the world of the *sidhe* and everyone in it. It was time to get on with what he could do and could control.

Bedwyr pointed to less well-lit spot, equidistant from the firelight at the center of the camp and the torches on the perimeter. "Your best bet is to run across the field at a crouch and fetch up between those two tents there. I'll be here when you're done, and if you don't return, I'll see to Penda's death myself."

"Good to know I'll be avenged when I'm on Arawn's rack." Hywel shot Bedwyr a grin he probably couldn't see and was off, crouching low as Bedwyr had said, scuttling across the field more like a thief than a knight. The Saxons had packed down the grass so it provided little cover. Hywel had to hope that the Saxons' night vision would be hampered by their own lights and the rain.

Ages later, but only a dozen heartbeats really, Hywel crouched behind the closest tent and then peered around it, still keeping low to the ground. Men bustled near a large tent twenty yards away.

Hywel straightened and adjusted his helm so it hid most of his face. He and Bedwyr had scavenged Hywel's entire outfit off a dead Saxon on the far side of the field. They hadn't had as many men to choose among as Hywel would have liked (far too many fallen Welshmen surrounded them) but the armor and helmet fit well enough. After this was over, he thought he'd hang onto his new axe, which had felt comfortable in his hand before he'd slotted it into his belt. He'd left his sword with Bedwyr, along with his surcoat sporting Cadwaladr's red dragon crest.

Hywel waited until the flow of men in and out of the tent subsided and then strode forward, Taliesin's parting words echoing in his ears, words that for once were clearly stated so that Hywel couldn't misunderstand: *Act like you belong there and know what you're doing. Nobody will question you. The men around you will see what they want to see: a fellow Saxon soldier.*

Loud shouts in Saxon carried on the breeze from the western end of the camp where Penda's captains gathered their men. Ignoring them, Hywel threw back the door flap and stepped into Penda's tent. The only light came from a lantern on a stubby table. Penda was alone, leaning over a map spread out in front of him, but looked up at Hywel's entrance. He looked back to the map, instantly dismissing Hywel, before bringing up his head again. "I don't know you."

"No, my lord," Hywel said in Saxon. "I have a message for you."

Penda looked past Hywel to the door of the tent, but none of his servants came through it. Hywel kept his hands loose at his sides, hoping that Penda wouldn't decide to run him through. He had a sword and Hywel wasn't accomplished yet in the use of his new axe.

"What is it?" Penda said.

Hywel bowed. "My name is Hywel. I bring you news from the King of Gwynedd."

"So Cadfael seeks peace, does he?" Penda said. "He snubbed my son, refusing him his wayward daughter. He has not responded to any of my messages and rebuffed my councils. It is too late for peace."

Hywel almost choked on his tongue. Could Penda not know that Cadfael was dead? That Cadwaladr was king? And yet, it appeared so. Hywel swallowed hard. This was not the news he'd thought he was bringing Penda. "My lord, I-I-I—" Hywel found himself stuttering.

"Why does Cadfael even bother with this charade? He must fear defeat. He must think he can turn his magician in my direction and I'll turn tail and run away. No." Penda shook his head. "I will crush Cadfael beneath my boot and all Wales will fall to me before the year is out."

Hywel finally marshaled his thoughts. "It is not Cadfael who sends you word. Cadfael is dead."

That seemed to shake Penda out of his complacency. He tsked through his teeth. "Not Cadfael? Then who? My sister never gave Cadfael a son. Who has taken the throne?"

"Your sister didn't need to," Hywel said. "She'd already given one to Cadwallon."

Penda's mouth opened in surprise. "The boy lived? I would have thought Cadfael was smarter than that. If I had been he, I would have scoured Gwynedd for every year-old son, just as Herod did in the Christian Bible." Penda laughed openly. "If all the rulers in that religion had his spine, I might join that faith myself."

Penda was definitely not the type to turn the other cheek.

"His name is Cadwaladr ap Cadwallon, soon to be High King of the Britons." Hywel's chest swelled at the thought. Here was a name—and a king—that could shake even this great lord of Mercia.

Penda's eyebrows furrowed. "You imply that because another man leads the Welsh, the game has changed? Why would I treat with him if I wouldn't have spoken to Cadfael?"

"Cadwaladr is your nephew."

"He thinks to bind me with blood?" Penda said. "I haven't spoken to my sister in fifteen years. Is that all you have for me?"

"King Cadwaladr sent me to warn you."

"Warn me? Enough of your riddles." Penda scoffed under his breath. "Give me your message and I might allow you to live."

"Oswin of Northumbria gathers a force on your northern border. If you do not withdraw from this fight, you may not have a country left to defend."

Penda crossed his arms across his chest and tapped a finger to his lip. "How does your king know this? Perhaps this is a trick."

"It's no trick," Hywel said.

"Withdraw, eh? He must be more afraid of me than I hoped, to think that such a ruse could possibly work. We outnumber you. You are locked in your little fort and cannot get out, with too few men to win the day. Or night."

Hywel kept his face impassive but Penda laughed again.

"I see I am right."

"You are wrong. King Cadwaladr sends me to you because he would prefer an enemy he knows on his border than one he does not. You might not die yourself today, but if you do not withdraw and turn your attention to Oswin, your army will never recover. You will not have the men to defeat him. And you yourself will not live out the year."

Penda stared at him and Hywel realized that his voice had changed as he'd spoken those last words, deepened into a rhythmic chant reminiscent of Taliesin. What had come over him? For Penda's part, he gazed at Hywel for several heartbeats.

"You resemble your father more than a little. Is he well?"

Another swallow. "He is," Hywel said.

"But the rest of your message is not that he comes to join me? To beg forgiveness for deserting me when I needed him most?"

"No," Hywel said. The word came out short. He forced himself not to glance towards the door, knowing that it would indicate weakness to Penda. Hywel had very little time. Bedwyr was waiting. From the looks of it, they still had a war to fight.

But Penda was done too. "Go. If I see you again, it will be your death."

Hywel didn't need to be told twice.

10

Rhiann

The Saxon torches sputtered and spit in the pouring rain, barely penetrating the cloak of darkness that had descended on Caer Fawr. Rhiann gazed over the rampart. Dafydd stood beside her, extreme tension in his shoulders. For Rhiann's part, she felt a strange sense of dislocation—as if what she was seeing wasn't real—and if it was, she was watching the scene from the point of view of someone else. The Saxons outnumbered them at least four to one. Maybe more. The defenders didn't have enough arrows. It was as simple as that.

Cade had told Rhiann about his argument with Dafydd. What Cade hadn't told Dafydd was that he'd listened, and had insisted to Rhiann herself that she keep as safe as possible. Whether or not Dafydd knew it, Cade was punishing him just a little by making him stay with her. They stood on a raised platform behind a palisade, overlooking the southwestern gate. By splitting their force to directly assault both gates at the same time, the Saxons had forced Cade to split his as well.

Rhiann was torn between horror at what was coming at them and an absolute refusal to believe that they were all going to die. If they couldn't hold the Saxons off long enough to prompt Penda to rethink this action, it would be hand-to-hand along the ramparts soon enough and there was no way the Welsh would win that battle.

"Aim for the neck or heart," Dafydd said.

Rhiann glanced at him. "I'm glad you've found Angharad."

"Can we not talk about it?" Dafydd said—and then proceeded to talk about it. "She's smart, and she doesn't talk too much, and she says she loves me. I have no idea why."

"Don't be foolish, Dafydd," Rhiann said. "I loved Cade before I met you. It doesn't mean you weren't worthy of love. Such modesty doesn't become you." She elbowed him in the ribs to take the sting out of her words.

"Remember Caersws?" Dafydd said.

"How could I forget?" Rhiann said. "I'm staring down at an overwhelming force where the odds don't favor us."

"And yet we won the day," Dafydd said. "Just the two of us."

"We did, didn't we?" Rhiann found courage at the memory, though that had been a different situation. These weren't mindless demons, chasing confused villagers across Powys. These men followed a commander who knew what he was doing and had won more battles in the last thirty years than any Mercian king before him.

"We have King Cadwaladr," Dafydd said. "Maybe they don't understand what that means."

"According to Hywel, they hadn't realized my father was dead," Rhiann said. "They are truly behind the times."

"Here they come." Dafydd raised his bow.

Because of the rain, they'd waited to tie their bowstrings until the last instant. As it was, the strings would soon be soaked and unusable. Rhiann had two spares. Like the arrows, she could only pray that they would be enough.

"They're coming!"

"Why didn't Taliesin save his explosion for now?" Dafydd said. "He could have killed two hundred of them instead of twenty."

"He bought us time." Cade said, coming to stand beside them, his own bow in his hand. Then, Cade lifted his voice above the grunting and marching of men. "Fire at will!"

Rhiann obeyed. At first, she focused entirely on the feel of the bow in her hand, the physical act of pressing and loosing arrow after arrow, and the concentration needed to aim it. She didn't even bother to see if her arrows hit anyone, so quickly did she reel them off. As it was, the Saxons were pressed so close together, accuracy was immaterial, and the first waves of arrows devastated the initial ranks of marching Saxons.

"Watch out!"

Cade launched himself at Rhiann and pulled her to the ground, cushioning her fall with his own body.

"What—what happened?"

"They have their own bowmen," Cade said. "I didn't expect it."

"They have one fewer now," Dafydd said.

Cade pushed to his feet but kept a hand on Rhiann's shoulder to keep her below the level of the rampart. "Stay there!"

He released six arrows in the time she could have gotten off one.

"Cade, this is ridiculous—"

"Not to me," Cade said. "And anyway, you can get up now. They're all down." He pulled her to her feet and into a quick hug, squeezed once, and set off at a run toward the rampart above them.

Rhiann went back to work.

It was a brutal business. Rhiann shot, and shot, and shot again, feeling that same welling up of fear—and the draining out of everything she cared about. As at Caersws, she became one with the bow, the string, and the arrow that she shot from it. She lost track of the number of arrows she loosed or the Saxons she hit.

Rhiann continued to shoot, mindful of her emptying quiver. Each archer had brought at least two dozen of his own arrows with him, but if Rhiann's were nearly gone so were everybody else's.

A call went up from the archers who held a more easterly position. "More arrows! We need more arrows!"

A moment later, Angharad appeared behind Rhiann and stuffed a handful of arrows into her quiver, and then more into Dafydd's.

"Taliesin is keeping count." Angharad's breath came in short gasps. "Take care of these. We don't have many left."

Angharad ran back to the stockpile.

"We've made headway against the Saxons, but how long can we hold out?" Dafydd said. He muttered under his breath, calculating the number of arrows, by the number of archers, by the Saxons they needed to kill.

His bow loose in his hand and unstrung, having run all the way from the northern gate, Hywel skidded to a halt behind Rhiann. "We've turned them back!"

"Are you sure?" Rhiann aimed carefully at a Saxon who had the temerity to creep into the ditch at the base of the wall below her. From what she could see, they'd only killed the first ranks of Saxons—not even a thousand men. And even that thought sickened her, knowing that she'd been responsible for many dozen all by herself.

"Hold!" Cade's call came from above them. "We can't afford to waste even one arrow." He landed beside Dafydd and Rhiann with a thud, having jumped the distance from the upper rampart. "Hywel's right. They've retreated from the northern gate. I don't know yet whether or not they intend to renew the assault there, or if they're going to concentrate only on this gate."

Rhiann lowered her bow. She didn't believe it. For every Saxon they'd killed, another had come to take his place. And yet, in the few moments she'd spent talking to Cade and Hywel, the Saxons below her had also backed off from the lowest rampart, to a point just out of arrow range, having faced just enough opposition to prevent them from laying their siege ladders against it.

"Maybe Penda is rethinking his decision to attack," she said.

"I don't think so." Dafydd pointed a finger which didn't actually tremble, even though a slight waver appeared in his voice. "The Saxons are bringing their wagons forward."

They peered together into the murk. "What's in them?" Rhiann said.

"Soil and ladders," Hywel said. "I saw them when I was in the Saxon camp. Penda must have been working his men like dogs to have managed this so quickly. He knows what he's about."

Cade waved to Goronwy who commanded the men in the portion of their defenses Cade had taken to calling 'the annex'. It was the bit of rampart that protected the entry gate on the southwest side of the fort, just below where Dafydd and Rhiann stood. "Cease firing! I need more bowmen on the first rampart. We must make each shot count!"

Rhiann pushed the sopping wet tendrils of hair that had come out of her braid out her eyes and gazed down at the oncoming Saxons with something that felt worse than horror. It filled her mouth with bitterness. The carts rolled right over the bodies of the Saxon dead.

"Is Penda mad?" she said. "Doesn't he see the carnage right in front of him?"

Cade wrapped an arm around her and pulled her to him. "He thinks to defeat us now, and that is worth any number of dead to him, if he can accomplish it before dawn."

"Surely doubt has seeped in by now," Dafydd said.

"If he finishes us off, he has no western flank to defend," Cade said. "He thinks he can handle Oswin as he has in the past."

"That we are defeated won't help him if he doesn't have an army left," Rhiann said.

"That's what I told him," Hywel said.

"Penda is an experienced commander. He will have realized that the pace of our arrows slowed, just before he withdrew his troops." Cade said. "In fact, that's probably why he withdrew. He knows that we are running out. He wants to give us time to contemplate our mortality."

"Would he honor a flag of truce?" Rhiann said.

"No." The three men spoke in unison, with no hesitation.

"And I wouldn't show one," Cade said.

Rhiann looked from one to the other. Each man had the exact same expression of grim determination on his face.

Catrin raced up to Cade, breathing hard. "Goronwy says one-third of his force protects the inner wall. If the Saxons crest the lower rampart, he'll be able to shoot them as they come up the pathway. But we need to take them down before they reach that point."

"Agreed." Cade lifted his own bow.

Side by side with Cade and Dafydd, Rhiann shot, and shot, and shot again. *Press. Loose. Press. Loose.*

But too many Saxons came at them. Now, for every Saxon casualty, two more came to take his place. The Saxons gradually filled the moat, even if the dirt they'd piled high in the carts was interspersed with the bodies of the dead. Another half an hour and the stockpile of arrows was gone. Each archer had a half full quiver, and was staring into a full frontal assault by the Saxons.

"Ladders!"

Two men holding the base of the first scaling ladder slammed it into the ground, while others swung it up against the rampart.

"Shoot them before they reach the top!"

But it wasn't really possible. The initial Saxon climbers fell but others took their places, swarming up the ladders like a waterfall in reverse.

"How many are there?" Rhiann said, her voice going high. She gazed across the wall at the oncoming Saxons.

No one answered her.

Dafydd tossed his bow to the ground and pulled out his sword. The Saxons had placed their ladders a few feet apart such that in total it seemed there were a hundred of them side by side.

Cade handed his bow to Rhiann. "Be safe, *cariad*. Get yourself to the hall. There's nothing more you can do here."

Rhiann stared at the bow. She clenched her jaw, wanting to deny him, but she felt Dafydd's eyes on her and knew it would be foolish to do so. "Yes, my lord."

Rhiann ran away. With every step she cursed and wept at the same time, tears streaming down her cheeks, hating to leave her husband and her friends but knowing that her skill with a blade would be inadequate to the task. She would only get herself killed along with them.

11

Goronwy

The first Saxon had just pulled himself to the top of the wall when an arrow pierced his neck. He screamed and tumbled forward off the ladder. Goronwy had a moment of relief, but shook it off the next moment. There was no hope here.

Another Saxon replaced the first, and then another, and surely there were hundreds more waiting at the foot of the ladder to take the place of those who fell. When the next Saxon appeared, Goronwy hacked him with a down sweep of his sword. He too fell back. And then so many faced him in succession Goronwy stopped counting.

Geraint moved up beside him and they fought back to back, in concert with the dozen other men who'd staked out this portion of the rampart. Goronwy knew many of them. He'd taught some of them sword play, but now, when it was no longer play, it was he they looked to for courage. As had been the case in the council hall, his lord was counting on him. Goronwy smiled grimly as he hacked away at another Saxon neck. He was better at fighting than talking.

On the other side of him, Bedwyr slashed at a Saxon who came up the ladder one over from the one Goronwy was protecting.

"To the wall!" Goronwy hoped they'd prove a bold sight to the other Welsh fighters, encouraging them to think they had a chance, even if Goronwy himself knew better.

He, Geraint, and Bedwyr leapt onto the rampart itself and swung their swords at the necks of first men who poked their heads over the top of the rampart. If Goronwy could maintain his position, he could stop every Saxon who reached the top of the ladder. The rain hindered both defender and attacker, making the sod wall of the rampart soft and mucky and the ladder slippery. More than one man's foot slipped off a rung and plunged him down onto the soldiers below him. It seemed every man tried a different technique for reaching the top, whether climbing one-handed with an axe in one hand, putting a blade between his teeth, or with a weapon slung along his back.

But none could reach the top of the wall more quickly than Goronwy could chop them off it. At the same time, not every defender was as skilled or as quick as these three and they didn't have enough men to replace those that fell.

Bedwyr cursed steadily beside him. At one point, Goronwy turned just as a Saxon came up behind Geraint and slashed at his head. Goronwy shoved at his friend and met the Saxon's blade with his own. But the few heartbeats he'd taken to protect Geraint had allowed a Saxon to reach the top of the ladder and leap down to the path behind it.

Goronwy swung around, panicked that he'd lost the rhythm of the fight. If he got behind the pace, the Saxons would overwhelm them. But in this instance, Bedwyr was there. Then once again, the friends fought together. As the moments passed, Goronwy lost track of all sense of himself, fiercely holding on with two hands to the hilt of his sword. He was aware only of the succession of blood-shot eyes of the Saxons in front of him.

"Retreat! Pull back!" The call came from the rampart above and behind them. The Annex had been a bold, initial line of defense, but they couldn't hold it.

Geraint obeyed instantly. Gorowny shoved his sword through a last Saxon, but then had to drag Bedwyr along the pathway towards the main gateway to Caer Fawr.

"Come on! Run!" Dafydd had posted himself at the top of the rampart above the gate and he screamed the words over and over as they ran.

"Loose!"

That was Cade from the level above, ordering the remaining archers on the inner rampart finally to release the arrows they'd saved. The barrage of metal held the Saxons back long enough to allow the exhausted Welsh to secure themselves inside the lower walls. The gate slammed closed behind them.

"Christ on the cross!" Bedwyr ripped at a strip of cloth from the hem of his tunic and wound it one-handed around a slit in his upper arm.

"Damn it! I thought we had them there for a while!" Goronwy said.

Goronwy sputtered and spit his anger, but after a skeptical look from Bedwyr, had to acknowledge that Cade was right to sound the retreat, and if he'd waited any longer, it might have been too late. None of them would have made it back.

Goronwy leaned against the inner wall and rested his head against the sod. Cade remained on the wall above him, shouting and pointing at men, one after another, each running off to do his bidding. From up there, he would have seen the heavy toll the Saxons took on the defenders.

Cade glanced down at Goronwy, who didn't even have the energy to lift a hand in acknowledgement of his king.

Cade jumped the distance instead. "You were the last to leave the balustrade, I see."

"We had to leave the dead and a few of the gravely wounded to the Saxons," Goronwy said.

Cade put a hand on his shoulder. "I know. Several of the men wanted to retrieve them, but I refused."

"The Saxons will slaughter the wounded," Geraint said.

Cade's face was drawn and as grim as Goronwy had ever seen it. "I know that too." He tipped his head to indicate the pathway that led to the gate in the second rampart. "Come. We have another wall to defend."

* * * * *

Goronwy and Cade ran up the pathway to the final gatehouse that protected Caer Fawr proper, this wall was ten feet higher than the lower one they'd been defending. The Saxon ladders wouldn't reach the top of that wall, no matter how many they crammed into the space. Possibly lashing two ladders together would do it, but whatever the Saxons decided it would take time—and give the Welsh time—to breathe until the Saxons regrouped.

"How many men have they lost?" Goronwy's breath was just beginning to ease. He glanced back towards the gate behind them. It held firm. *For now.*

"Many, but a lower percentage than we have," Cade said. "I had hoped that Penda would have reconsidered by now."

"He wants you dead, my lord," Goronwy said. "Whether or not you're his nephew. Family ties are nothing when they give no advantage to him."

Cade grunted, not necessarily his assent, Goronwy thought, but his understanding. Ahead of them, the rest of the stragglers passed through the higher gate, inset into the inner wall, that protected the next level of the fort. Goronwy and Cade were the last.

"Hurry!" Geraint waved at them from above the gate. He held a bow, ready to shoot at the Saxons as they leapt off their scaling ladders and onto the path behind the now undefended rampart.

Just as they turned into the doorway, Goronwy checked behind them one more time. A wiry Saxon had crested the wall to Goronwy's right. He whipped out a bow from its rest at his back—

"Watch out!"

—and loosed a shot at Geraint whose attention was elsewhere.

The cry stuck in Goronwy's throat. The arrow hit Geraint full in the chest. He folded over it and fell forward off the rampart, plummeting the thirty feet to the pathway below. The Saxon gave a cry of triumph, and suddenly two dozen Saxons were at the top of the wall and leaping down to the pathway.

"Inside!" Cade shoved at Goronwy, who couldn't move for shock. "I'll get him!"

Cade raced to Geraint's crumpled form while Goronwy screamed at those who guarded the gate to keep it open, even as the Saxons seized on their inattention to try to beat them to the open door in the inner wall. Goronwy planted himself in front of the gate and with a flurry of sword strokes fought three of them off long enough for Cade to slip through behind him.

Once they were safe, with the gate slammed shut, Cade laid Geraint against the wall near the great hall. The arrow was grotesque as it protruded from his chest, and his eyes sightless.

"I can't help him." Cade eased to his feet as he stared down at Geraint. "He's gone."

Goronwy rested with his head in his hands. Then, filling his lungs with air, he tipped his head back to gaze up at the sky. The rain had stopped just after they'd retreated to the second rampart and a few stars had come out, interspersed among the clouds. They had perhaps two hours to dawn.

"If it affects our next course of action, it looks like the morning will dawn clear, Cade," Goronwy said.

Cade nodded. "It would, today of all days. But that actually makes the decision easier, doesn't it?"

12

Cade

"Get up!" Cade toed Dafydd's prone form with his boot.

"I'm awake!" Dafydd had fallen asleep with his back to the wall. He sat near other archers who'd come through the doorway and collapsed to fall asleep where they lay. Angharad lay curled up next to him, her head on his thigh. The sky had lightened. Somewhere it was dawn, but the sun hadn't yet peeked over the eastern horizon. "How long have I slept?"

"Not long enough, I'm sure," Cade said. "There'll be plenty of time for sleeping when this is over, or none of us will ever sleep again."

Dafydd stroked the hair from Angharad's face and wiggled his legs to get her to wake up. She sat up, gazed at Dafydd with a completely blank stare that told Cade she wasn't really awake. She then leaned back against the wall and closed her eyes again. Dafydd got to his feet.

"I apologize for earlier, my lord," Dafydd said. "I said some things I shouldn't hav—"

Cade held up his hand to stop him from speaking further. "Two friends had a difference of opinion. That is all. That's not what this is about." At the same time, he was glad that, like him, Dafydd hadn't wanted to let the argument fester.

Dafydd blinked, opened his mouth, and then closed it. Cade knew how his friend felt: confused but too tired to try to guess what Cade wanted.

"I have many noble men among my companions," Cade said. "But only one has ever held the sword of the White Hilt. That man is you." Cade had been holding Dyrnwyn, hidden in a borrowed sheath with the belt wrapped around it, behind his back. He brought it out and showed it to Dafydd.

"But I thought it wasn't the real Dyrnwyn?" Dafydd gazed at the sword in clear disbelief and didn't take it.

Cade stepped closer and lowered his voice. "We were mistaken. Put it on."

"You want me to wear it?"

"Wear it and wield it. At first light, we ride. We will scatter the Saxons before us—and you will lead the men."

"Why not Goronwy? Or you for that matter? With Caledfwlch and the cloak you can fight in the sun, just like you did yesterday—"

"With the cloak, I am invisible, and Caledfwlch along with me," Cade said. "How do I lead my men when they can't see me? If I tell them that I am fighting among them, they will follow you."

Dafydd stared at the sword. Cade didn't urge it on him, just held it out to him. As far as Cade was concerned, the decision was the right one and the more he thought about it, the more sure he was. But Dafydd had to come to that himself, for by accepting Cade's challenge, not only would he lead the men, but make himself the center of all the action on the battlefield. A man had to choose that, not have it thrust upon him unwilling.

"Go ahead." Angharad spoke from behind Dafydd and he turned to look at her. She pushed to her feet and came to stand beside him, her hand on his arm. "I don't want you to fight, but given that you will whether I want you to or not, you should be the one to carry Dyrnwyn."

Dafydd gazed down at her for a long count of five. Then he turned to Cade. "I will do it."

"I'll be the unseen hand beside you." Cade clapped a hand on his shoulder. "Ready yourself. We ride in within the hour."

Cade walked away from Dafydd and Angharad, leaving them to sort themselves out as they saw fit. Back inside the hall, he found Rhiann consulting with Catrin. "I need to speak to you, Rhiann," Cade said.

Rhiann gave him a long look in which he read more understanding than he necessarily wanted. "I already know what you're going to say."

"And what is your answer?" he said. "I know you're as skilled in the use of the bow as any of us here, but I can't let you fight this time—not from the walls—not with the chance that the Saxons will come over them."

Rhiann gazed at him steadily.

Cade tried again. "Enough men have already died today without losing you."

"What do you want me to do?" she said. "Defend the retreat again?"

"There will be no retreat," Cade said. "Every man capable of sitting on a horse—and that means every man here—will ride out to face the Saxons. You, the other women, and the servants, will remain inside the keep. If the Saxons get this far, we will all be dead and Caer Fawr will be theirs. If I am dead, Penda will spare your lives."

"Are you sure about that?" Catrin said. "Why would he?"

Cade stared past her, unseeing. Penda would spare Rhiann so he could marry her to Peada, but Cade couldn't bear to say that. "So Taliesin says," he said.

"He's awake?" Rhiann said.

"Awake and insisting he is well, for all that he's lain unmoving on a pallet since I brought him inside."

"A temporary thing only," Taliesin said.

Cade turned and couldn't help smiling to see the bard crossing the floor of the hall with long strides.

"Rhiann and I will watch from the top of the keep," Taliesin said. "We will be able to see the action well enough from there."

Cade looked down at Rhiann. "I saved some arrows, just for you, Rhiann. You'll have an even dozen, plus the one that Arianrhod left you."

Rhiann took the quiver from him, looked down at it, and then back up at him. "I suppose you didn't have to be a seer to see this coming."

"If you do end up needing them, make them count."

"I always do," she said.

"Ach, Rhiann, how can you laugh?" Cade pulled her into his arms. "I fear the world is ending, and we with it."

"I don't believe it," she said. "I can't believe it." She hugged him once, and then with a whirl, she strode away, Taliesin beside her, heading for the stairwell that led to the top of the keep and the battlements that would allow them to keep watch on the course of the battle.

Cade gazed after them. And then Catrin gasped. "My lord! Rhiann is—" She bit off the words.

"You do have a gift, then," he said. "For I saw it too."

"I saw two heartbeats where there should be only one," Catrin said.

Cade put a hand on Catrin's shoulder. "Tell her for me, if I don't survive this day. She will have a future King of Gwynedd to live for and protect."

"Of course, my lord." Catrin's voice trembled as she spoke, and then firmed. "Is that what you fear? Has Taliesin seen it?"

"Taliesin will not say."

13

Goronwy

Goronwy steadied his horse and pulled up beside a man who had a swath of blood coating his chest. Earlier, he'd been bleeding out on the floor of the hall.

The man saw Goronwy inspecting him and shot him a beatific grin. "Rhys ap Morgan was my lord. I'd followed his father since I became a man, and then him." He gave a short laugh. "I've died twice today already, and been resurrected by King Cadwaladr. Now I'm alive and well again, and about to die for a third time."

"King Cadwaladr doesn't actually bring men back from the dead." Goronwy checked the front of the line to see what kind of time he had before they would ride. Dafydd mounted his horse and leaned to the right. It looked odd until Goronwy realized that Dafydd was listening to Cade, though neither man, sword, nor horse were visible.

Cade had promised to act as a guard for Dafydd, and that was the only reason Goronwy hadn't tried to prevent it, or laughed at the absurdity of his brother leading their host of men. Goronwy still had trouble seeing his brother as a man, much less a knight upon whom all depended.

"Doesn't he?" the man said. "If Rhys had listened to him perhaps I would never have died at all." He moved away and fell into line on the right flank of the line of men.

The pathway down from the main gate was so narrow that only two men could ride abreast in places. Goronwy found a spot in the left column, and then Bedwyr pulled up beside him on the right.

"I like her," he said, by way of greeting.

"Who?" Goronwy said.

"Angharad. I like her. Your brother chooses well."

Goronwy coughed a laugh. "I do too, though I find it disconcerting that my little brother has such a way with women. Angharad has already helped him forget Rhiann."

The two men glanced to the top of the keep, where their queen stood behind the balustrade with Taliesin. The risen sun shown full on their faces and Rhiann shaded her eyes with one hand. Meanwhile, Taliesin held his staff aloft. That had Goronwy scoffing again—or almost—before he swallowed it. Who was he to question whether Taliesin's entreaties would do them any good? The world of the *sidhe* was far closer to this one than Goronwy was comfortable admitting.

Dafydd stood in his stirrups at the head of the company. He held Dyrnwyn above his head and Goronwy hoped that only his closest companions noted how white his brother's knuckles were around the hilt. Suddenly, the sword burst into flame from hilt to tip.

"We ride!"

Goronwy thought the call came from Cade, though the roar from the men that followed drowned out his certainty.

A shout echoed throughout the courtyard: "Hail Cadwaladr! King of the Cymry! The King shines forth!" Sure enough, the glow that even the cloak couldn't hide suffused Cade's position, Dafydd, and the half dozen men around them.

The gate opened and they urged their horses forward. The narrow causeway between the ramparts was full of Saxons, milling about uncertainly. They must not have understood the words the Welsh had shouted, or if they did, not understood what they meant. Several of the ladders from the outer ramparts had been brought forward, but the short while Cade had given his men to prepare wasn't enough for the Saxons to organize their attack.

The riders swept down the pathway, their arms swinging and their horses taking out every Saxon within reach. With each foot they progressed, they picked up speed. All the way down from the fort, the hapless Saxons fell under the hooves or—those who were less lucky—to one side, where a Welsh sword sliced through them. At the front of the line, Dyrnwyn rose and fell. Many of the Saxons succumbed to Cade's invisible sword as well.

Those ahead of Goronwy had killed so many Saxons, that Goronwy found himself with little to do. Until he swung around the corner of the last rampart, past the Annex that they'd fought so long to defend, and straight into the bulk of the Saxon army on the field that hadn't yet channeled between the ramparts.

"My God!" That was Bedwyr from beside him.

Just ahead, Hywel checked his horse, which gave Bedwyr and Goronwy time to flank him. Dafydd and Cade cut a swath forty yards in front of them, still buttressed by nearly twenty knights, but the hundreds of Saxons had slowed their momentum. The three friends exchanged a glance, and in half a heartbeat, they all understood that their heroic charge had been exactly that: heroic, but ultimately fruitless, even if the immortal King of Gwynedd rode at their head.

Against all expectation, Goronwy's heart lightened. He threw back his head and laughed, and then spurred his horse into the fray, with Hywel and Bedwyr close behind. Even if this meant his end, he would die with his friends on every side, and wouldn't be among the living when the Saxons finally overran his country. He prayed that the Saxons would spare the women as Cade hoped, though Goronwy himself had no such expectation. Then he put everything from his mind but his sword and the men he intended to kill with it.

He met a Saxon axe with his blade and ripped it away. He turned to the other side and thrust the point through another man's throat. But then a third man buried his axe in his horse's chest and he went down. Goronwy cleared his feet from the stirrups, leaping just in time to a vacant spot of what had once been grass. Back to back with Hywel, with hardly a pause for breath, he continued to fight.

Goronwy lost track of the men he'd killed; lost track of all of his friends but Hywel. Sweat poured down his face, from the effort, rather than the heat of the day, since it seemed that the promise of sunshine had been a faint one. Better for Cade, perhaps, were he to lose the cloak. Better for Rhiann standing on the battlements. Goronwy glanced upwards. In the time since they'd left the fort, clouds had massed above them, dark, black, and menacing.

Only from the light that still shot from the center of the field did Goronwy know that Dafydd and Cade were alive. The light grew brighter, almost blinding him with its intensity when he looked towards it, and still the Saxons didn't give way. Goronwy shoved his sword through the midsection of one Saxon, pulled it from his belly and in almost the same motion, slashed through another's thigh. He spun, meeting a third man's blade. The Saxon's red beard covered his face and a grin split it. For the first time, Goronwy felt weakness in his arms and found himself giving way under the onslaught.

And then the point of an arrow punched through the man's ribs. The Saxon had been lunging at Goronwy, his axe held above his head, readying for a killing blow. Now, he stared down at the arrowhead that seemed to come from nowhere. Goronwy looked past him. Rhiann had shot him from the top of the keep.

He wanted to shout at her, to tell her that they were a lost cause and that she was to save her arrows for the last end of need. Which forced into his mind the sickening thought that maybe they'd reached that point, that Rhiann had seen the end coming and was prepared to use her last arrows if they would give her friends a few more moments of life. Behind him, Hywel still fought as one possessed and

Goronwy resumed his place, at his back. Sweat mixed with blood ran into Goronwy's eyes, and he swiped at it with the back of his hand.

Or maybe those were tears.

14

Dafydd

When Cade had offered him Dyrnwyn, Dafydd hadn't taken it. Standing before his king, he'd felt like someone had stuffed cloth inside his skull, like Angharad's pillow, he was thinking so slowly. But now—now that he was on the battlefield—he'd never felt more glorious than he did in this moment.

He didn't know if it was the sword, his position at the head of the company, or that King Cadwaladr rode beside him, bringing down one man after another. Dafydd fought as if this was the only reality he would ever know. His sword flaming higher than ever, Dafydd followed its lead, as if it had a mind of its own and Dafydd was a slave to its will.

Saxons scattered before him and he envisioned himself fighting just like Cade had fought against the demons outside Caer Dathyl. He would turn and they would flee before him; they would throw themselves upon their own blades; Taliesin would compose songs to his greatness...

"You're getting too far ahead."

Cade's sharp rebuke brought Dafydd back to reality. He didn't let up the motion of his sword arm, but it was like Cade had thrown a bucket of cold water over his head. He could sense everything around him again and was no longer wrapped in a muffling wool that prevented his senses from working. He felt it all: his muscles clenching and unclenching, his knees signaling to his horse, the ache in his shoulder from the effort of wielding the sword, the whistling of the wind through his helmet, with a high-pitched whine until he wanted to rip it from his head at the incessant noise.

"This way," Cade said.

Cade had been giving orders all along as they fought. Dafydd had just been ignoring him. Now, he did as he was told, working his way back towards their own men, instead of following a suicidal course towards the center of the mass of Saxon men.

Nonetheless, Dafydd had allowed too many Saxons to get between him and the Welsh line and because of it, three Saxons converged on him at once. Though he took out one, and Cade another, the last sliced through the meat of his thigh.

The pain was so unexpected, he screamed. To make matters worse, his moment of inattention allowed a fourth

Saxon to bury his axe in his horse's neck. The horse went down and Dafydd just managed to leap free.

"Stay with me!"

Dafydd's stomach curdled at how exposed they were, even if the push and pull of battle had ebbed for the moment around them since Cade had severed the neck of three Saxons in succession to get to Dafydd. He gaped at the blood that poured out of his leg and he scrabbled with his free hand to stop the flow.

And then to Dafydd's horror, Cade dismounted and ripped off the invisibility cloak. He held out Caledfwlch. "Trade me."

When Dafydd looked at him stupidly, Cade thrust Caledfwlch into Dafydd's hand, took Dyrnwyn from him, dropped the invisibility cloak over Dafydd's shoulders, and pinned it around his neck.

"Will it heal me?" Those were the only words Dafydd could think to say.

Cade planted his feet, his back to Dafydd and his power shining out. It reflected off the black clouds above them, even if he wielded less than he might have were it night.

"Damn well better," Cade said.

And even as Dafydd watched, his wound closed. Another dozen heartbeats and he could stand and take his place, back to back with Cade, though this time it was Dafydd's sword that was invisible and he who dispatched would-be attackers who thought they would take out the King of Gwynedd from behind.

In truth, for all Dyrnwyn's glory, Dafydd was glad to fight with Caledfwlch instead. She didn't require some kind of test to wield her, and even if she wasn't as mighty as Dyrnwyn and didn't flame from hilt to tip, she felt more comfortable in his hand.

"I'll want her back when we're done here," Cade said, reading Dafydd's mind. "And the cloak."

Dafydd's heart lightened further when a moment later, from three different directions, Bedwyr, Goronwy, and Hywel appeared to join their circle. They were invincible now, no matter how many men came against them.

"Hold!"

The command echoed around the field and the Saxons obeyed, falling back from Cade's ring of men. Even Dafydd's countrymen faltered. Stunned, Dafydd saw a man wearing Hywel's crest remove his helmet and sit on it, his head bent and his sword lose in his hand. No Saxon took advantage of his capitulation because the Saxon warrior beside him did the same thing.

Through the faltering forces strode two dozen men in black. They converged on Cade's small ring of five from every direction. Dafydd barked a laugh at how unsurprised he was at this turn of events. Part of him had been expecting something like this from the start. Mabon was late to the party, but that didn't mean he wasn't eventually going to show.

"I thought we killed them." That was Bedwyr, deadpan as usual.

"Apparently not," said Hywel, having obviously spent too much time in Bedwyr's company.

"They killed King Arthur on the road to Caer Fawr," Goronwy said.

"And the men of Castell Clydog, back in Ceredigion," Dafydd said.

"They are here now; that is all that matters," Cade said. "And if they are here, then Mabon can't be far away."

The five companions backed towards each other, narrowing their circle so fewer of Mabon's men could attack them at once or isolate them, one from the other. The first man to appear in front of Dafydd was clean-shaven, his nose a fine point. He didn't see Dafydd, of course, since he was invisible and that was all Dafydd noted of him before Caledfwlch skewered him through the belly. Dafydd didn't remember even thrusting the sword.

But he didn't have time to think about it before another set upon him. And another, and he lost track of anything but these men in black who shouldn't be here, and yet were.

He'd killed four men and had countered the blade of a fifth when he sensed commotion to his right. He strained to see what was happening out of the corner of his eye, while still taking care of his opponent. Dafydd managed to dispatch him, and then turned to see Cade holding off two men at the same time. One was enormous, built out of solid rock it seemed, and the other was Mabon.

Sick to death of Mabon and all the damage he'd done, Dafydd moved towards Cade, stumbling over a body on the ground as he did so. Cade held out a hand, however, to stop him, despite the fact that Dafydd was still wearing the cloak so Cade shouldn't be able to see him. With that motion, it seemed like the entire battle slowed, just for this moment. Maybe it was some new magic of Cade's. Perhaps Mabon was disturbing the passage of time. Dafydd pulled up just behind Cade and glared at Mabon, but the god had eyes only for the King of Gwynedd.

"Put up your sword. You have lost." The familiar sneer was plastered to Mabon's face.

Dafydd opened his mouth to deny Mabon's words, but then couldn't. Where earlier Dafydd had seen Welshmen and Saxons sitting together, now they set upon each other again. Every man moved so slowly, however, it was as if their swords weighed a hundred pounds. Right in front of him, a Saxon killed one of Tudur's men. Gagging, Dafydd looked away, towards the west and Caer Fawr. The castle was in flames. Tears pricked his eyes.

A moan came from behind him. He spun towards it, terrified of what he might find, and it worse than he'd imagined. Goronwy lay on the field, about to lose his head to one of the men in black. Hywel and Bedwyr were already down.

"No!"

Dafydd threw himself at Goronwy's attacker. He wrapped his arms around his waist and brought him to the ground with his full weight. As they hit the grass, the fall knocked Caledfwlch from Dafydd's hand, but he didn't care. He sat up, straddled, the man, and punched him in the face. The man tried to defend himself, but Dafydd gave him a sharp cut that broke his jaw and Dafydd's hand.

"Dafydd!"

The word came sharply and again, because it was the voice of someone he loved, he came to himself. Goronwy had crawled to the spot where Dafydd had dropped Caledfwlch and fallen flat on it.

"Thank God," Dafydd said.

He staggered to where his brother lay healing from the gash Mabon's man had put in his side. Dafydd collapsed next to him and swung the invisibility cloak over both of them. Goronwy would live. Many wouldn't. Dafydd swallowed his tears at the loss of his friends, and put one finger on the top of Caledfwlch's hilt. His broken hand began to heal. But from this battle, the Welsh would never recover.

15

Rhiann

Rhiann fired an arrow, adding to the carnage in the fields below Caer Fawr. Wind had whipped around them almost from the instant the battle started and chilled her to her core. The battle raged right in front of them, right in front of the lowest rampart. The main Saxon force had gathered in the field on the near side of the little creek. Penda must have thought they would soon be entering the fort, once they'd figured out how to breach the final rampart.

Her heart rose to her throat as she watched, such that she could hardly breathe around it. Taliesin had remained beside her as the morning wore on and the number of bodies of the fallen, already too numerous to count, grew ever larger. It was easy to think *why doesn't he* do *something*, but Taliesin's magic could not save their army.

She'd seen, long before the men possibly could have, that the Saxons were going to win. She shot another arrow at a man who'd been about to decapitate Hywel. Every time she aimed her bow, her hands trembled in the moment before she fired. She had to swallow hard and still them, trying to capture the calm that was required for the task. And failing. But then all of a sudden, she knew what to do, and she wasn't going to do it standing here, too far from the fight to see it properly or make a difference.

She ran for the doorway to the keep. Taliesin grabbed her arm but she shook him off. "I'm not close enough. Stay or come, I don't care which."

She barreled down the stairs from the battlements, skidding down each step since she was moving so fast. Taliesin came on behind her, no longer protesting. Rhiann burst into the great hall. A dozen women looked up as she entered—mostly camp followers and hangers-on—along with Angharad and Catrin, who lifted a hand to her as she passed them.

"What—" Angharad said.

Rhiann waved back, not wanting to alarm them since it would do no good. She simply told them the same thing as she'd told Taliesin: "I need to get closer."

It wasn't that she couldn't shoot an arrow four hundred yards. Of course she could. Even with her smaller bow, she could make one fly that far. But accurate? She'd almost killed Hywel with that shot. She'd never been so nervous to loose an arrow in her life, not even at the battle at Caersws where she and Dafydd and defended the retreat of the women and children.

Maybe she'd been naïve then. Maybe she hadn't known enough. Now she did, and it brought her to her knees.

Rhiann crashed open the door leading from the great hall, passed a few men who'd made it back inside the fort, and headed for the gate. The door had been left partially open and she ran through it.

"Rhiann, it isn't safe—" Taliesin said.

"Safe enough," Rhiann said.

Taliesin let it go, since they were already on the path. As she'd seen from her position on the battlements, the Saxons who'd surged between the ramparts in their initial victory had been decimated by the Welsh charge. Those that remained had given up trying to get into the keep. Their ladders didn't reach, and the battle had moved outside. The Saxons had gone with it, unaware that the Welsh hadn't even bothered to close the door.

At last she reached the Annex—the defense works that Goronwy had defended in the initial assault. It had a twenty-foot high rampart, augmented by walls that encircled an area fifty feet wide and twenty deep. Though it protected the main gate at the bottom of pathway, once the Saxons had come over the walls and opened that gate from the inside, they'd abandoned it as a post.

Taliesin closed and barred the gate to the annex, effectively locking them into this small, raised haven amidst the turmoil below them. The ancients had built it for just such an occasion, if the annex was all that was left of a defense, rather than the keep.

Rhiann climbed to the top of the wall. If anything, the roiling mass of men had moved closer to the ramparts in the time she'd taken to get here. Twenty feet away, a Welshman lost his head to a Saxon axe. She'd seen so much carnage, it shouldn't have surprised her, but tears sprung to her eyes anyway. She brushed them back.

Goronwy, Bedwyr, Hywel, and Cade, who'd thrown off his cloak, stood in the center of the battlefield. Rhiann didn't see Dafydd and her heart fell, until she realized that he must be filling the gap in their ring. The companions fought in a circle, their backs to one another facing outward, as a phalanx of attackers in black surrounded them.

She turned to Taliesin, her gaze imploring. She couldn't help it. Druids had spoken to the gods for thousands of years and he was the only one with any answers here at all. "Are you sure—"

"This is a long way from over."

But for once, Rhiann didn't believe him. Couldn't believe him. He'd been right so many times before, but ...

"Stand your ground, Rhiann, and don't waste your arrows," Taliesin said.

"I'm almost out."

"I'll get you more." He left her to scavenge arrows from the quivers of the dead archers who had fallen in the initial defense of the fort.

Rhiann set her feet and began loosing arrows into the Saxon army. *One, two, three* ... She trusted that Taliesin would find replacements, and as promised, before her remaining ones were spent, he appeared beside her with fistfuls that he stuffed into her quiver.

She had to pause in her shooting as he filled it, and their eyes met. A light grew behind Taliesin's eyes that she hadn't seen since that day they'd met, months ago on the battlements of Dinas Emrys. Taliesin then stepped away. He raised hands above his head and focused all his attention on a point over the center of the battlefield where Cade and his friends fought.

Earlier, at the start of the battle, he'd chanted words she couldn't understand, but now he lifted his chin and his voice rang out above the howl of the wind and the clash of men:

A knight on a swift horse
creates turmoil among his enemies
Thither will come an ancient enemy,
Grief will he know.
Sin and treason follow
And old hatreds are renewed
One stroke of his sword
And our war-lord comes
He remakes us
and brings to us a new Eden.

And as Taliesin finished, the most beautiful sound Rhiann had ever heard came from the west, wafting across the hills and fields. It was a horn. Not a Saxon horn, but an old-fashioned Welsh one. She knew the sound, even knew the horn, though she'd only heard it once before, in the setting out from Bryn y Castell before the ride to Caersws. A lifetime ago.

Rhun, Siawn, and their men had finally come.

With their coming, the storm that had threatened to unleash its rain, ever since their men had ridden out of the fort, broke over the battlefield.

Wind and rain whipped into her face as Rhun's men crashed into the side of the Saxon lines. What had been a cohesive force collapsed. Rhun's sword rose and fell, slaying every man within reach. But there were so many, and Rhun had two hundred Saxons to fight before he could reach Cade and his friends. The hope that had briefly flared in Rhiann's heart drained out again, even as she shot one arrow after another, refusing to stop until either there were no more Saxons, or she ran out of arrows. Then to her horror, the ring of fighters broke apart. Every one of Cade's men had gone down, and Cade himself faced a last man alone.

Except it wasn't a man. She couldn't see his face, but she knew that stance. She knew that glow that emanated from him and told her the god confronted her husband again.

Mabon.

How she hated him.

Taliesin put a hand on her arm. "You see him? That means it's time."

Rhiann swept her rain-soaked hair out of her eyes and raised her bow. Lifting her eyes to the heavens for one last prayer, she focused all her attention on this last chance for some kind of victory. Her hands trembled and her wet bowstring didn't respond as it should. She would have replaced it earlier if she'd had any to spare. But even so, she pressed the black arrow, the one she'd been saving, the one that Arianrhod had given her by the river, into it—and then loosed it.

It hit Mabon in the center of his mass.

And with that shot, power exploded in the center of the field. It burst from the place Mabon had been standing and surged outward like waves from a boulder lobbed into a pool of water. The force pushed men and horses with it, laying them flat to the ground as it passed. It reached Caer Fawr and blew past and through Taliesin and Rhiann, who herself was thrown backwards off the top of the rampart.

Rhiann came to herself, flat on her back below the wall. Her bow lay ten feet away. Even Taliesin, whose composure had never wavered throughout their vigil, was on his knees, though still on the top of the wall.

He reached down a hand to her. "You'll want to see this."

Coughing, she got to her feet and clambered back to Taliesin's position. The field lay before her, still rain-soaked, though the downpour seemed to have lessened slightly. The five companions stood together. Cade held Dyrnwyn point down, its fire out.

Here and there, the Saxons they'd been fighting staggered to their feet, their swords and axes forgotten. Rhiann's jaw dropped to see half as many as there had been a moment before. Cade himself reached out a hand to a helmetless Saxon soldier to help him to his feet. Even from this distance, Rhiann recognized him by his ornate armor and the black swath of beard across his face. He'd visited Aberffraw when she was a girl. It was Penda, the King of Mercia

"What has happened?" Rhiann said. "Where did all of Penda's men go?"

"The gods fought with us and against us," Taliesin said, "just as I had foreseen."

"I don't understand," Rhiann said. "Mabon ..."

"He is gone for now, as are his troops."

"But he had no demons at his command," Rhiann said. "We faced real men."

"And almost were overcome by them," Taliesin said. "But as with the *glamour* he affects in our world, the size of the Saxon force was an illusion. Penda had many men, but not as many as we believed. If Penda had defeated us, it would have been in part because we defeated ourselves. We believed Penda had thousands more soldiers than he did."

"But we lost so many men!"

"Did we?"

"But Rhys! And Geraint!"

Taliesin nodded. "Yes, they are dead, but look around you now and tell me what you see."

Rhiann had a hand to her mouth. Many of the men who lay on the field of battle were dead, but here and there, men stirred and shook their heads. Could it be they'd received blows from which they were only now recovering? Could so many really still live?

"I don't believe it!" Rhiann said. And then the tears began to fall in earnest as all her fears and hopes coalesced into a potent mix of joy and pain, sorrow and gladness. They hadn't lost all their men. Wales would not be left defenseless. Her heart rose in her throat, along with hope. "But—" Rhiann swallowed and tried again. "And the arrow I shot at Mabon? Is he truly dead this time?"

"Arianrhod's arrow, his mother's arrow, ripped away the glamour and the links that anchored him to our world. My hope is that in Mabon's moment of weakness, Arianrhod would have tied him to her in the world of the gods. She couldn't find him—couldn't contain him—and was relying on you whom she deemed worthy to find him for her. If what I believe is true, he is trapped now in his mother's keeping."

"But for how long?" Rhiann said.

"That I cannot say," Taliesin said.

Rhiann stared at Taliesin for a long count of five, and then threw whatever caution she still had—which wasn't much to begin with—to the wind that roared down the valley from the west.

The battle might have been over, but the storm hadn't spent its fury. The rungs of one of the ladders the Saxons had left propped against the rampart were slippery. She almost fell off at the end and landed hard. Once on the ground, it was difficult to see past Rhun's men and horses, but most of the men had dismounted by now and she found a path through them to Cade.

He hadn't seen her coming so when she launched herself at him, she almost knocked him over. But he weighed more than she did and he steadied himself, lifting her off the ground and clutching her to his chest. "*Cariad...*"

"I didn't see how we could win," Rhiann said into his collar. "It seems as unlikely now as it ever did."

"So this is the girl who has caused so much trouble."

Rhiann turned in Cade's arms. Penda stood before them, his hands loose at his sides. "I'm the girl who causes trouble?" she said. "Who encroaches on our lands with every day that passes? Who took advantage of my father's death to—" Rhiann broke off, so angry she couldn't finish her sentence.

Cade whispered in her ear. "Mabon visited Penda too, weeks ago."

Understanding dawned in Rhiann. She narrowed her eyes at the King of Mercia. "He told you that you could win."

Penda bowed. "As you say."

And that was all the apology they were going to get. The Welsh had fallen again and again to the Saxons, but rather than live under a foreign rule, they'd retreated west, into Wales. Penda had waged a war against his own nephew, over rocks and trees he didn't care for anyway and would have had a hard time controlling even if he did win.

Penda eyed Cade now. "Your emissary told me the truth about Oswin of Northumbria?"

"He did," Cade said.

Penda surveyed the battlefield. "I suppose you wouldn't consider fighting beside me against him? You've not lost as many men as you feared. You would be welcome."

Rhiann gaped at him, but Cade answered civilly. "Better an enemy I know than one I don't, is that it?"

Penda shrugged. The gesture was so dismissive—so casual—as if none of what he'd done mattered, that Rhiann wanted to launch herself at him like she had at Cade, except she would then scratch his eyes out. All he cared about was his own power and if Cade agreed to fight beside him—as Cadfael and Cadwallon had before him—it would be a victory of a sorts.

Cade studied him, still not answering, and Rhiann was struck with a sudden vision of Penda, lying on a field in the sun, his lifeblood flowing into the grass from a wound to the gut. She'd never *seen* before, but this felt like a sudden truth. If Cade denied Penda's request, he would not live out the year, just as Taliesin had foretold.

"I'm sorry, Uncle. I cannot fight for you today," Cade said.

16

Cade

Cade sat behind his desk, gazing at the chess piece Rhiann had brought him, turning the little king around and around in his fingers. The knife and the whetstone were to one side, and the cloak in a chest behind him. Dafydd still had Dyrnwyn in his possession and Cade had seen no reason to ask him for it.

A cold anger still burned in Cade that he'd needed to use it, and at how close Cade had come to winning the battle but losing the war. If all had happened as Mabon desired, Cade's army would have been so weakened and diminished, it would have been left open to an attack from anyone who could marshal enough men.

But once Mabon was gone, the *glamour* he'd created had vanished. The veil had lifted and the trauma of the day had lessened. Cade had reached Bedwyr and Hywel soon enough to help them. Them and others, through the power of Caledfwlch. Many hadn't lived to fight another day and Cade mourned the loss of every man. Still, he had to be grateful that there were fewer widows to accuse him with their grief.

"I'm glad that Caer Fawr wasn't really on fire," Rhun said.

"*Glamour* again." Taliesin closed the door to the room, stumped over to a bench set against the far wall, and settled himself onto it. "I would give much to ensure a way to see through it."

That was quite an admission, coming from Taliesin. Cade gestured in the general direction of the hall, where his other friends were dining. "So many were sorely wounded. That was no lie."

"I for one, dislike intensely that I cannot trust my own eyes," Rhun said. He'd turned his chair around and sat with his arms resting on the back rail, cushioning his chin with his fists.

"Even I can't see through it," Cade said. "Maybe that's the next gift I will ask of Arianrhod."

"I wouldn't," Taliesin said.

Cade laughed under his breath. "No more gifts, eh? I suppose that's wise."

The three friends fell silent. In the aftermath of the battle, Taliesin and Cade had already talked for hours about the gods, about the battle, about the war that could rage in the world of the *sidhe* if Beli and the *sidhe* council learned of Mabon's actions. And at this point, how could they not?

Cade pointed to the Treasures in front of him. "What are we going to do with these now?"

"With Mabon gone, do we need to worry about them?" Rhun said. "Arianrhod has him contained, right? Isn't that what you said, Taliesin?"

"It is," Taliesin said.

"But for how long?" Rhun said.

Taliesin grunted his assent. "That is the question."

"We have to assume the worst," Cade said. "And plan for it."

"And that means collecting the Treasures ourselves," Rhun said. "If nothing else, it will spare their owners the danger inherent in them."

"And the cup of Christ?" Taliesin said. "Your holy grail of Christendom?"

Cade glanced at his friend. "You know about that? Underneath Dinas Bran you said it was *just a cup*."

"I didn't *see* as clearly then," Taliesin said. "It isn't one of Mabon's Treasures, but surely it is one in its own right."

"The monks say it bestows immortality on those who drink from it," Cade said. "Just like the drinking horn in your poem."

"You could go get it," Taliesin said. "Give it to Rhiannon."

Cade's eyes narrowed. Rhiann was asleep in the room behind them. In the weeks since Caer Fawr, her pregnancy had taxed her strength such that she slept more often than she was awake. "And keep her with me always? Of course I want that, but it would not serve."

"You could ask her," Taliesin said.

"You're tempting me," Cade said. "And I will not be tempted."

"As you say." Taliesin sat with his staff propped against his shoulder, gazing down at the floor. The workman had come a long way on the project of restoring Dinas Bran to its former glory. Another month and they'd finish the curtain wall. Provided nothing happened in the interim to stop the work.

Cade fingered some of the papers on his desk, the Treasures always at the edge of his vision, as if individually they might leap up and talk to him at any moment. He took a deliberate breath and let it out. "Will you find the rest for me? I need to know how close Mabon was to his goal to unite them all. We must know where they are and if they are safe."

Taliesin bowed his head. "You are confirmed in the idea that you won't keep them for yourself, then?"

"Of course," Cade said.

Taliesin nodded. "If you had not given me this task, I would have asked for it." He walked to the table and picked up the sacred knife from its spot.

"And the dark force that rose from the cavern?" Cade said. "You have not mentioned it since we rode for Caer Fawr, but I can see that it haunts you."

"It is pure evil," Taliesin said. "The druids have always drawn their power from the earth itself, but not all power is good. And some of my kind spent too much time in the dark." Taliesin met Cade's eyes. "I will be careful."

"Please do."

"I will attend your crowning at the summer solstice, my lord."

"I will expect you," Cade said.

Rhun stood too. "He wouldn't really be High King if you weren't there to keep him humble, would he?"

Cade shared in the laughter and sketched a wave as Rhun left the room.

Silence. Taliesin and Cade gazed at each other. Their eyes said a great number of things that they chose not to put into words.

Finally, Taliesin spoke. "I leave you in good hands."

"I'll try not to be too reckless in your absence," Cade said.

That brought a rare smile to Taliesin's face. "Blessings upon you, and upon your House, my lord."

And he was gone.

Blessings upon my House. Cade rose to his feet. Political power had come to him through right of birth and strength of arms. Love, however, was something that could only be earned. Something else that Mabon would never understand.

Cade followed Taliesin out the door and turned toward the room he shared with Rhiann. *His House.* He had a wife and child waiting for him.

Historical Background

The 'Dark Ages'—the era in which *The Last Pendragon* is set—were 'dark' only because we lack historical material about the period between 407 AD, when the Romans marched away from Britain, and 1066, when William of Norman conquered England.

For Wales, the time was no more or less bright than any other. The relative peace the Romans brought was predicated on the brutal subjugation of the British people. When the Romans le the Britons faced the Irish from the west, the Scots from the northwest, the Picts from the northeast and 'Saxons' (who were Angles and Jutes too, not just 'Saxons') from the east. To a certai degree, it was just more of the same. The Britons had their lands back—the whole expanse of what is now Wales and England—for about five minutes.

It does seem that a ruler named Vortigern invited some Germanic 'Saxon' tribes to settle in eastern England, in hopes of creating a buffer zone between the Britons and the relentless invasions from Europe. This plan backfired, however, and resulte in the pushing westward of successive waves of 'Saxon' groups. Ultimately, the Britons retreated into Wales, the only portion of land the Saxons were unable to conquer.

The rule of Cadwaladr ap Cadwallon sits at the resting point between the Welsh retreat and the Saxon advance. As romanticized by Geoffrey of Monmouth, he was the last Pendragon, the last King of Wales before the Cymry fell irretrievably under a wave of Saxon invaders.

With Cadwaladr's death, the battles began again, and continued through the Norman conquest, to the lonely death of Llywelyn ap Gruffydd in 1282 AD, thus ending, for the next 700 years, the dream of an independent Welsh people.

Cadwaladr ap Cadwallon

What little is known about Cadwaladr ap Cadwallon comes from a few texts. As I write in *The Last Pendragon*, upon the death of his father in his first year of life (634 AD), Cadwaladr was hidden from the man who usurped the throne of Gwynedd, Cadfael, only to return at the age of twenty-two and regain his father's crown.

He is mentioned in the following sources:

The Harlaein Genealogies: a collection of old Welsh genealogies preserved in British Library, Harleian MS 3859.

They've been dated to the reign of Hwyel Dda (10th century). Cadwaladr is mentioned as the son of Cadwallon and the father of Idwal, all Kings of Gwynedd.

Annales Cambriae (the Annals of Wales): A single line: 682 - A great plague in Britain, in which Cadwaladr son of Cadwallon dies.

Historia Brittonum: This text was composed sometime between 828 and 830, attributed to Nennius. Of Cadwaladr ap Cadwallon, he states: "Catgualart (Cadwallader) was king among the Britons, succeeding his father, and he himself died amongst the rest. He slew Penda in the field of Gai, and now took place the slaughter of Gai Campi, and the kings of the Britons, who went out with Penda on the expedition as far as the city of Judeu, were slain."

The Book of Taliesin: Taliesin was a Welsh poet born in the mid to late 6th century. Two poems that mention Cadwaladr are attributed to him. One is *The Great Prophecy of Britain* in which he rails against the Saxon incursions and praises the rule of Cadwaladr: "Cadwaladr is a spear at the side of his men; In the forest, in the field, in the vale, on the hill; Cadwaladr is a candle in the darkness walking with us; Gloriously he will come and the Welsh will rise ... " (my interpretation). The second is the *Prediction of Cadwaladr*, which is incomplete. It speaks of Cadwaladr, not Arthur, as the one who sleeps in the mountains to return at the nation's greatest need.

History of the Kings of Britain: This is Geoffrey of Monmouth's romantic and fanciful tale, telling the supposed story of the history of Britain from its founding by Brutus to the death of Cadwaladr.

Myth and Religion

The blend of Christianity and paganism that I write into *The Last Pendragon* is my take on what it might have been like to have been religious in seventh century Wales. While many fictional accounts of the Dark Ages describe conflict between pagan religions and Christianity, that seems to be a product of the medieval mind, rather than an accurate analysis of Dark Age religion. For there to be conflict there must be a power relationship as well as organization, and for both the pagans and the Christians in Wales at this time, there was little of either.

When the Romans conquered Wales in 43 AD, although Rome was not Christian at the time (Emperor Constantine didn't convert until 311 AD), the legions systematically wiped out the reigning religion of Wales at the time, which was druidism. Why did they do this? The Romans themselves were pagans, with a pantheon of gods and goddesses. Why did they not simply associate the native gods with existing gods from their religion as they did in most other places, and as the Catholic Church did with its saints later throughout the world?

The difference was that the druids formed the basis of a nationalist movement in Britain—and throughout the Celtic world. To quell it, the Romans systematically destroyed the sacred sites and groves, particularly on the island of Anglesey, prompting Boudicca's revolt in 61 AD. The Romans defeated her, and the end of the revolt spelled the end of organized druidism in Britain.

Thus, in the time between this momentous defeat and when the Roman empire became Christian, there was a lengthy vacuum, both in religious leadership and belief. Christianity came to Britain in the first century, not long after the death of Christ, but was no more organized than paganism without the druids. Wales was far from Rome and the seats of learning, and when the Roman legions left, the Christian religion was cut off from its roots. Christianity in the Dark Ages, then, was one of several available options in Wales. By the mid-600s, the time period of *The Last Pendragon*, Christianity was growing more organized, but it was a religion based around monasteries. There were cells of monks and hermitages, but few, if any, churches as we understand them. There were also strong pulls towards different sects within Christianity, and strong resistance to the Roman Church, with which the Welsh Church did not reconcile until 763 AD.

Even up until the death of Llywelyn ap Gruffydd in 1282 AD, the Welsh Christians were unhappy with conformity to Rome, especially as the Church kept excommunicating their Princes for not bowing to England. Welsh laws did not conform to the Church's teachings well into the Middle Ages. Most notably, women in Wales had a higher status compared to the rest of Europe, divorce was easier, illegitimate children could inherit, lords levied fines instead of executing criminals as punishment for crimes, and the punitive forest laws of English/French feudalism were absent.

Religion in the Dark Ages was at the intersection of superstition and mythology. The old Welsh gods had not been vanquished, but were everyday participants in daily life. They were random and capricious, just like the weather. Jesus Christ brought a message of personal salvation and belief in heaven, rather than the Underworld. Christ allowed a believer control over his ultimate destiny.

Eventually, it was Christianity that associated the pagan Welsh gods with its pre-existing pantheon of saints, accommodating the old beliefs. In the *Spoils of Annwn* by Taliesin, a Christian, (a poem which I have adopted for *The Last Pendragon*) the final two stanzas of the poem rail against dissolute monks, comparing them to wolves or wild dogs and end with a prayer to the Lord and Christ. At the same time, the bulk of the poem describes Arthur's descent to the Underworld and his battles in the world of the *sidhe*. This blend of pagan and Christian is the hallmark of Dark Age Wales.

Acknowledgments

I have many people to thank, not only for their assistance with *The Last Pendragon Saga*, but who have helped make my books better and my life sane for the last ten years.

First and foremost, thank you to my family: my husband Dan, who told me to give it five years and see if I still loved writing. Ten years on, I still do. Thank you for your infinite patience with having a writer as a wife. To my four children, Brynne, Carew, Gareth, and Taran, who have been nothing but encouraging, despite the fact that their mother spends half her life in medieval Wales. Thank you to my parents, for passing along their love of history.

Thanks to my beautiful writing partner, Anna Elliott, who has made this journey with me from nearly the beginning. Thank you to the many support groups to which I belong (you know who you are).

And thank you to my readers. You make it all worthwhile.

About the Author

With two historian parents, Sarah couldn't help but develop an interest in the past. She went on to get more than enough education herself (in anthropology) and began writing fiction when the stories in her head overflowed and demanded she let them out. While her ancestry is Welsh, she only visited Wales for the first time while in college. She has been in love with the country, language, and people ever since. She even convinced her husband to give all four of their children Welsh names.

She makes her home in Oregon.

Made in the USA
Las Vegas, NV
16 March 2022